Praise for JT LeRoy and *Sarah*

"One of the unfortunate casualties of the JT LeRoy saga was the career of Laura Albert, a tremendously gifted and empathetic writer who found herself overshadowed by her own creation. But long after the media frenzy died down, the stories endure— harrowing, haunting and heartfelt tales that speak with the sort of raw, devastating honesty that can seem almost impossible to muster without a pseudonym. It's thrilling to finally have Laura's stories liberated from JT's story, and to have Laura and her words back together again."

—Adam Langer, author of *Crossing California*

"I can't think of any other presence in lit like JT LeRoy, one who upon mere appearance completely redrew the lines between author and art, persona and myth. Even better is rediscovering years later how boldly and bewitchingly these words trace out their somehow ghostly landscapes of desire and debris, and therein, in their essential beauty, how alive the mystery actually still is."

—Blake Butler, author of *There Is No Year*

"LeRoy manages to write simply about the most tangled of emotions—and to describe, without hatred or self-pity, the most monstrous of deeds."

—*Newsweek*

"Wildly imagined, but described with a quiet sureness . . . *Sarah*'s considerable originality testifies to LeRoy's wonderful ability to make up beautiful thin

plement

D1642805

"[LeRoy is] a hungry writer with the instincts of a person who fishes to eat. Once he hooks the reader he doesn't let go   quick, lively, and fascinating."   —*Bookforum*

"JT LeRoy's masterful imagination, command of story, and easy sense of the mythological are a rare combination that demands attention."   —*Toronto Star*, Sunday book section

Sarah

Sarah

a novel

JT LeRoy

corsair

CORSAIR

Originally published in 2000 by Bloomsbury
This edition published in the UK by Corsair in 2016

1 3 5 7 9 10 8 6 4 2

Copyright © 2000 by JT LeRoy.

The moral right of the author has been asserted.

A CIP catalogue record for this book
is available from the British Library.

ISBN 978-1-4721-5258-9 (paperback)

Printed and bound in Great Britain by
Clays Ltd, St Ives plc

Papers used by Corsair are from well-managed forests
and other responsible sources.

MIX
Paper from
responsible sources
FSC **FSC® C104740**
www.fsc.org

Corsair
An imprint of
Little, Brown Book Group
Carmelite House
50 Victoria Embankment
London EC4Y 0DZ

An Hachette UK Company
www.hachette.co.uk

www.littlebrown.co.uk

For Trevor

Sarah

Glad holds the raccoon bone over my head like a halo. 'I have a little something for your own protection,' he says, leaning down over me so close that I can't help but stare up at the brown patches of skin that mottle the pure whiteness of his face.

'Glad, you look like you're sharecroppin' out your own private patch of cancer,' some of the lot lizards would tease him. But I know the truth of it. Glad told me himself. It's the Choctaw in his blood. That's why he's got good medicine. That's why he's a good pimp for a lot lizard to have.

'These patches of brown be the In'ian in me, making themselves known,' he tells me over a trucker special breakfast at The Doves Diner: a huge mound of hollandaise eggs and thick-as-a-Bible persimmon pancakes. I know he wants me to work for him. His stable is known for being the finest from coast to coast. Glad's little bits don't have to stand outside the truck stop like other goodbuddy lizards usually do. Truckers call in to arrange their appointments months in advance. All Glad's pavement princesses dress so comely in the most delicate silks from China, fine lace from France, and degenerate leather from Germany. If you didn't notice them wearing a raccoon penis bone necklace, and if you didn't know what that meant, you'd never know they were actually male. Most of his boys are either runaways rounding up some cash before heading out with some driver one of these days, or they are like me, have family working the main lot. Nobody bothers with Glad's boys. Some of the lizards say it's because he pays off anyone that would ever have a say. Sarah told me it is because all the ex-con truckers make sure they have Glad's finest boys to look forward to and the local law wouldn't want to start no riot by depriving felons of their sweet reminders of the penitentiary. But I know it is because of the raccoon dick.

He holds it over my head.

I lean down and let him slip the rough-cut leather cord around my neck. I always see Glad's boys in the diner, fingering their coon pricks in a real show-off way. They never have to pay their checks. I always hear the waitress saying when she puts in the boy's order, 'It's for them two of Glad's with the mountain man toothpick.' And a bill never comes.

The lizards say Glad just pays their tab like any sugar daddy. Sarah says all the waitresses secretly are in love with Glad and his boys so they don't charge them. But Glad tells me it's neither. 'They know most of their business is hungry tricks that work up their appetite after a visit with my boys, and they count on my boys leaving their tricks in a generous and lavish mood.'

'This better than a policeman's badge,' Glad says as he adjusts the necklace over my black sweater. I knew he was going to give me my bone today, so I borrowed a black sweater from Sarah.

'Gettin' boned today is what I heard,' she called from inside the bathroom of the little motel room one of her regulars on the green-bean run pays for. I knew she was soaking in the shower.

'I don't care how cheap the room and the hoe, a woman needs a soak same as a coal miner.' She clogged up the drain with wet menstrual pads and towel-lined the shower rim to add an inch or two to her bath. She sat in the corner huddled like an orphan in a flood with the shower pouring down. 'You'll be soaking your pump knot in here too once Glad puts you out.'

I went through the always half-packed plastic attaché case and picked up her black sweater. I pressed it to my face and inhaled her familiar scent of stale cigarettes and alcohol ineffectively masked by powder-scented air freshener.

'You better not swipe my leather skirt,' she yelled over the shower water streaming down.

I leaned into the Sheetrock bathroom door. 'I'm going as a boy,' I shouted.

I heard her make a 'that's what you think' laugh. I kicked the door and it shook harder than I'd meant. 'You ain't the first person to kick in this door.' She laughed and I felt relieved she didn't come after me, but more than a little pissed she didn't even take me half serious enough to try to whip me. It's 'cause she's in her soak, I told myself. I could smell the baby powder scent of her bubble bath and felt excited to come home after a long night of trucker lovin' and deserve my soak just like she did. She never let me use her bubbles. 'Buy your own when you work your own!' she'd tell me when she'd see me fingering the bottle covered in pictures of naked baby bottoms.

'I'm coming home with some of my own bubbles!' I shouted into the door.

'And leave the keys till you pay me half this rent.' Her voice raised some and that gave me a tinge of pleasure and fear. I grabbed up the black sweater and opened the front door. I walked back over to the Sheetrock bathroom door and said as loud as I could without yelling, 'You don't even pay for this room your own self, but since I'll be making more than you *As a boy*, I'll kick you down some change.'

Then I ran. Heard her pulling herself up before I finished. I slammed the front door and didn't even look back once.

'This bone stands out nice against your sweater,' Glad says after he is done adjusting it on me.

I turn and look in the plate glass and there it is, on me, yellowish white like tobacco chewers' teeth. I always wanted to glide my fingers along its curvaceous lines.

'Shape always 'minded to me like half a waxed moustache . . . how they get it in their women's privates is all but beyond me,' he says with a snort, and some unswallowed Kentucky coffeetree drink sprays out at me.

I carefully wipe the Kentucky coffeetree spray off my face. I've heard truckers talking in low voices how Glad is known to have murdered a few drivers that did his boys a bad turn. He did it with his coffeetree drink, some in the know say.

'It would only be a Yankee with no manners or sense of self-pride that would hurt a young defenseless boy trying to make a night's wages,' I once heard Big Pullsman Todd say between forkfuls of his Wellington of king salmon with truffle mashed potatoes. 'Yankee drivers,' about ten other truckers swore and spit in their spittoons that were fixed directly a foot and a half to the sides of each of their booths. Most would usually miss and make spattered lizard designs on the fake marble with sparkles in its linoleum.

Every now and then a trucker would sit in the diner and boast of busting up a faggot goodbuddy.

They didn't notice how the room went quiet. I heard it said that one northerner sat there laughing, wearing one of Glad's boy's raccoon bones around his own neck. He didn't look up from his medallions of chicken-fried Ahi when the boy came in—face bruised and misshapen like a sat-on plum, Glad at his side. The boy nodded in the Yankee's direction. Glad sent the boy into the arms of Mother Shapiro, the den mama, to one of his caravans he kept for the boys with no homes of their own.

I heard that the noise got louder as everyone made a show of acting real regular so they could claim themselves so engrossed in the conversations going on, they never noticed anything foul afoot.

But everyone heard the song. It has its place in the middle of the jukebox, an inconspicuous number as any: 24B. The A side is worn out skipping 'Bad, Bad Leroy Brown.'

Everyone made a show of not watching Glad walk real slow, through the swing doors and into the kitchen. Via the open order station window, everyone pretended not to be looking at Glad taking off the leather thong around his neck and removing one of two identical leather pouches he wore next to the hugest raccoon penis bone anyone had ever seen. Bolly Boy stopped checking on his tuna-noodle soufflé and took the pouch from Glad. It was well known Bolly had once been one of Glad's boys, but retired when he fell in love with a john that drove a custom. He swore he'd be true, but he was so used to giving pleasure to all the truckers he was sure his pledge would be in vain. But Glad fixed him with a job as a chef and paid for chef lessons, so Bolly Boy could stay chaste and still deliver pleasure, which made everyone happy. Bolly's sous-chef, Paxton Maculvy, was another one of Glad's who retired when he fell in love with the faces the drivers made when consuming the creations Bolly made. 'No trick ever rolled his eyes to heaven like that when eating me,' Paxton sighed. So Glad sent him to chef school, but on account of Paxton being illiterate, he dropped out and studied with Bolly in the truck-stop kitchen instead.

The Yankee never noticed the corners of all the truckers' eyes following Paxton as he strode over to the jukebox and used a special key to open the box up. If Bolly hadn't been such a great chef, the northerner might've had a chance to take a break from his side dish of liver with crème fraîche strudel. He could've taken note of the subtle hush in the diner as Paxton fingered his coon penis bone with one hand while pressing the buttons to put song 24B on for ten continuous plays. If Bolly had been less of a chef, the Yank might've done more than just hum along unconsciously to the old TV song theme blasting from the juke. He could've recognized that, like an Indian war whoop warning before the attack, the *Davy Crockett* song was being played. If the calf liver reduction sauce on the fresh corn ragout had been a little off, he might've got the mental picture every trucker had in the diner. Davy Crockett in his raccoon hat. He might've lit a wet rag out of that diner and escaped with his life.

The place almost jumped when Bolly himself, with his raccoon prick hanging almost in the Yankee's face, bent over to set down with a thud a pecan flambé and lit it up with a flash at the man's table. Before the Yank could protest that he had ordered no such thing, Bolly whispered in his soft voice, 'This, sir, is on the house.'

The Yank never would've thought that was the last conversation he would ever have in this world. Everyone's eyes were pretending not to be on the flambé, so the steaming brown coffee mug Bolly casually placed next to the pie was paid no mind. And only the folks that knew what was in Glad's leather pouches knew that it was the steaming brown mug that would do the Yank in and not Bolly's work of art pecan soufflé. Though again, if Bolly had been less of a chef and the soufflé not as dense, yet airy and so sweet you couldn't help but roll your eyes to heaven and give a praise of thanks, well, the Yank could've had a chance to notice that the coffee had a distinctly strange flavor to it. If he had been a local he might have recognized that he was sipping on a coffee substitute made from the seeds of the Kentucky coffeetree used by poor miners. If he had been a botanist he might have known that unless those seeds and leaves are roasted to a crisp brown, they are as poisonous as a deep mine with a broken vent. The Yank had to sip his coffee against the richness of Bolly's dessert. Somewhat immediately he started to get a stomach cramp, but there were still pecans, shiny in their sugar web, to be fished out of the white goblet, so he ate greedily through the discomfort.

The talk got extra loud as the truck driver from up north wearing a stolen love bone too tight around his neck paid his check and left for his truck. Everyone noted, as they watched him climb into his cab, that the man was bowed over some, rubbing his stomach as if it were a genie lamp.

The Department of Health and the sheriff made a visit to the diner not long after they found the northerner's stiff body curled up in a fetal position in the back of his vomit-festooned cab. He was pulled off to the side of the Interstate for a day and night before the highway patrol found him. It was the raccoon prick bone around his neck that brought the sheriff in and the crumpled napkins saying The Doves Diner that brought in the Health Department.

The sheriff nodded as he spoke to one of Glad's boys that wore no bone. The boy, through spit-wet eyes, told him a tale of love and a gift he had made to the Yankee. The Health Department collected mouse droppings and Roach Motels so full they could be used as maracas. The sheriff tried to comfort the boy and handed him back his bone. The Department of Health shut the diner for seventy-two hours and gave it a several-hundred-dollar fine. No one ever noticed it was Glad who paid the fine. And no one ever said a word about the known fact that Bolly's kitchen was kept so clean that when he invited many a trucker to eat off of his floor, many took him up on it.

Nobody ever said a word about it. Except in hushed tones of gossip you could overhear if you had good hearing.

I subtly finish dabbing up the Kentucky coffeetree droplets off my cheeks. I knew Glad had never hurt one of his boys, even when he had reason to. But I couldn't for the life of me tell the difference between the two pouches around his neck. What if he made a mistake and didn't notice he had Bolly make his mug from the pouch that held the unroasted seeds and leaves?

'You live with family? In the Hurley motel, don't you?' Glad asks, blowing in his mug and accidentally spraying me again.

'Yes, sir.' I nod and pat my face with a napkin. I'm not sure what Sarah is supposed to be to me so that's all I say and Glad says nothing more on it either.

'I've seen her working the lots. Pretty lady. I'm sure she does well.' Glad nods and I nod. 'Girls, 'specially pretty blonde young girls, can do themselves quite a turn.'

I look down at my bone again. I hope everyone saw him putting it on me. I don't think it would be exaggerating to say I heard a dip in the volume when he did—not as much as when Glad murdered the Yankee, but along those lines somewhat.

'I heard it said you look fetching in a leather miniskirt yourself,' Glad says.

Sarah used to dress me up herself. She would do my makeup. I loved watching her lick her finger and run it gently under my eyes. It always reminded me of those nature films of a mother bird regurgitating food into its baby's mouth and left me feeling as full as if she had. When we'd go shoplifting, it was better for me to be a girl, even if I couldn't be as pretty as her.

'Girls have more cubbyholes to hide things in,' she'd say, shoving cigarette packs down my dress and into my empty bra and cold wet chopped meat into my panties. 'Men only want to stuff those with themselves—they don't ever see what we hid in 'em!' She'd laugh at the guards staring at our legs and I laughed with pleasure at being included in her 'we.' But she'd stopped dressing me even though it's easier to make your way in the world as two girls. Easier when you're sitting at a diner, loudly fretting over only having enough for a Jell-O salad when a baconburger would go down real nice, to get a man to lean down over you and say, 'Let me take care of this, little darling.' Easier to get invited to stay the night at a man's place instead of sleeping in the car. Most anything you want in this world is easier when you're a pretty girl. She stopped letting me dress when it got too easy for those men to crawl from her bed into mine.

But I didn't stop. Sometimes I would put bows and sparkle gel in my curly shoulder-length hair until it shimmered, just like Sarah's. Now and then, when I knew she had gone with a trick to gamble out on a delta boat, I would wander the tic-tac-toe-like board lines between the trucks and act like a new girl, a new dress for sale, out on the stroll. I kept to the dark and ran if a john or another lizard called to me. I showed enough to make them interested in who this mysterious girl could be. I thought no one ever saw me enough to know it was me. I convinced myself I was like a comic book hero, hiding in the shadows, my magic stiletto heels clicking away all evil. I watched the lizards climb in the trucks and I giggled to myself as the cab suddenly started a-rockin' and a-rollin' till the lizard would just as abruptly leap from the truck stuffing dollars in her boot. I only got whipped once for using Sarah's things and that was 'cause I was sloppy and she found me out. I had stepped in a deep puddle, and because I had stuffed newsprint in her shoes so I could walk in them, I lost my balance and fell. I broke her heel and put a bad stain and tear in the fine leather of her skirt I had paper-clipped high around me. I tried to get it fixed, but she noticed right off. Before that no one had ever told on me. But folks knew. Glad tells me how much the men are all of fond of seeing me dash under the lamplight like a forest sprite. Even the girls think it's sweet, and that I would make an excellent lizard for real. That was what had brought me to his attention.

'Those divine golden curls of yours are very much admired,' Glad says, with a raise of his eyebrows and a sweet bowing of his head; asking my permission to touch them.

I lean forward and tilt my head like a cat under his caress. 'Soft as pig belly.' I almost fall flat on the table pressing my head into his hands.

'You'll be my guest when you dine here, so maybe you can fleshen up some. Our customers tend to like a little meat on their girls.'

I thought of Sarah saying, 'I told you so!' So I say to Glad, 'I could be a boy too. I know what to do.'

'Lots of boys want to work for me.' Glad takes my hand and genteelly holds it. 'What a man looks for in a boy is a lot different than what he looks for in my boy-girls.' He flips his long braid past his shoulders. I squint at him to try and see the Indian in him. He always spoke about being Indian, but aside from his long black braid and his facial spots, I can't see it.

I heard it said that his hair isn't really black anyway. It's just hair-care-product black. His eyes are too blue, even though he tries to downplay it with his heavy lids, keeping them half closed. His nose is flat, more like an Irishman's than like an Indian's. But the story is, his great-grandmother or maybe it was his great-great- or great-great-great-grandmother was a Mississippi Choctaw. No one knew which, not even Glad himself. Mother Shapiro was the only one that had seen the truth of it. She is the oldest and wisest lot lizard at any truck stop in any state, and it is widely known that the sheriff visited her trailer every now and then. She was a long time ago from the North, but no one holds it against her. She likes Sarah. I'd often see Sarah and her cuddled up in one of The Doves' booths. Sarah would lean in against Mother Shapiro's Hawaiian Muumuu-covered mounds of flesh and eat banana crème brulée while Mother Shapiro stroked her hair curls.

'His name is Glading Grateful ETC . . . The ETC is in capitals with three dots after the ETC sitting there like a trail into the sunset,' Mother Shapiro had told Sarah as they sat in Mother's round bed snuggled under goose-down blankets from Hungary. Sarah told me all about it. And I knew she was trying to make me jealous, so I pretended not to listen and kept saying, 'What? What?' until Sarah did stop and I had to beg her to tell me what Mother told her.

'Mother Shapiro saw an authentic copy of Glad's driver's license,' Sarah finally continued. 'The Sheriff showed it to her because he couldn't believe anyone would put ETC and three dots in a name just because he don't know how far back the first Glad was.' Sarah loves to tell gossip when she is drunk. Even if she had sworn to hate me forever, if she found out any information about anyone at one of the bars she always stopped at after she was through for the night, she would talk to me. I watch all the gossip shows to arm myself with material.

Sarah was on the bed, her head between her spread-out legs to keep from puking. But it didn't keep her from telling me what she'd learned from a night with Mother about Glad's Great-Grandmother ETC . . .

'A missionary devoted his life to taking her from a Choctaw to a Christian. He gave her lessons on how she could put Christ's joy and love into her heart.' Sarah rolled her head up and down in a little vibrating laugh and I knew it was a move she copied from Mother Shapiro. 'So he went about gladdening her and making her grateful and . . .' She laughed and let her whole body shake as if she were round and undulating like Mother. 'Glading Grateful the First was born some nine months later.'

I moved myself slowly till my side was next to Sarah's arm and I cautiously let my head rest on her shoulder. We sat there in the dark of the room, occasionally lit up too bright by the glare of a truck heading out. I slid my feet under the nubbly bedcover, slowly like a crab under sand, to be next to hers. And we stayed like that until we both were asleep.

'Well, I would like very much to have my own skirt of leather and my own makeup bag that closes with Velcro,' I say to Glad.

'I can get you a big sight more than that,' he says and thumps the table.

We start my training right away in the caravans back behind The Doves. I try to tell Glad I know what to do, that I've been with enough of Sarah's boyfriends and husbands, that if they had paid me I could buy a gator farm. Glad tells me I have to unlearn bad habits learned by watching drunken whores, no disrespect intended.

'You have to learn to read a man and know when he's just lookin' for fun and when what he really needs is for you to hold him so he can cry his eyes out like a babe,' he told me as we drank strawberry Yoo-hoos and sat on custom satin-covered bean-bag chairs. 'You have to learn how to listen. There is medicine in that penis bone to help you learn how to love like a real professional.'

I take daily lessons from various boys of Glad's, who affectionately refer to each other as baculum, which Glad tells me means 'little rod' in Latin.

I practice rolling a condom on a man with my teeth without him knowing. I practice how to take every bit and grain of a man in my mouth. I already knew that one. I'd have contests with Sarah. We'd lie on our backs side by side on some motel bed, with our heads hanging, tilted back over the edge of the bed, till our mouths, esophaguses, and throats would all line up. Then we'd put in a carrot as deep as we could without gagging. We'd mark the carrot with our top teeth and after we'd see who was the better head-giver. Sarah always won.

'You win 'cause you're older and bigger,' I told her once and she slapped my face so hard I saw stars.

'Don't you ever call me old and big,' she said and ran out crying.

I acquire tricks, like spraying Binaca on your right hand, so if a date is not on top of his hygiene, you can breathe in the scent of fresh mint from your hand and think of the snowy Alps instead of inhaling his ammonia scent and being reminded of a dirty Porta-Potty.

I learn how to trick with men who want to dress in lacy frilly things.

'That's the most difficult one,' Pie tells me. Pie was born a woodscolt—a bastard, and half white on top of that. To his Chinese mother from a traditional Chinese family that ran the only traditional Chinese restaurant in the upper reaches of the Appalachian Mountains, it was a disaster. They tried to keep him hidden by making him tip long beans and slice bitter melon all day and night. All Pie wanted to do was be a Japanese geisha, and as soon as he was old enough he hitchhiked all over, ending up in San Francisco. He came back home when his Great-Aunt Wet Yah was dying. His Great-Aunt Wet Yah was the only one who let him wear her silky undergarments and read to him from a forbidden book on the great geishas she had happened to possess. Wet Yah died and now Pie was working for Glad, saving up to move back to San Francisco and open his own geisha training school for men.

'You have to listen very carefully when you are with a man

that wants to dress.' Pie uses his hands while he talks, gracefully waving them back and forth as if he were icing a cake in the air. 'He might only want to show you how nice he looks in his pink panties and discuss how much he enjoys the feel of the smooth material against his privates. Or he might want to be a lesbian and make love to you as a woman making love to another woman.' Pie moves his body in a flowing S, making the silk of his kimono ripple so sinuously as to suggest two women making love. 'Or the gentleman might wish to be called a little sissy pantywaist, teased and otherwise humiliated.' Pie shakes his hips and mimics a femmie boy. 'You can often make extra by making the gentleman pay to bring in other bacula to laugh at him.' I nod and scribble notes in a notebook Glad has given me.

'The gentlemen often do not tell you what kind of crossdressers they are. You have to listen and take their clues.' Pie sits down on a beanbag and looks at me studiously, the slight slant of his eyes accentuated by broad strokes of black liquid liner. 'It is your job to figure out: do they want to pretend you are a woman completely, do they want you to be sweet and gentle, do they want you to be forceful and fill their hungry mouths, do they want abuse or gentle guidance? The faster you can figure this out, the more famous you will become.'

And Pie is famous. Cross-dressers come from as far away as Antigua to see him. But I don't need to be told which boys are the best. All I have to do is look at the raccoon bones around their necks. The better the whore, the bigger his bone. I heard it said that the bigger bones aren't real, that Glad just melts waxed dental tape onto a small bone until it is bigger. I look at Pie's and it looks authentic. Big and genuine.

'You're ready for your first date,' Glad says to me two months after I've started my training. I haven't lived at the motel room in a month. I stay at the caravans. Sarah took off with a rich crooked cargo inspector, and I check the room every day to see if she is back. The plastic attaché case is gone, but her bubbles are still there in the bathroom so I know she'll come back eventually. I plan to have my own bubbles on the shelf next to hers by the time she gets back.

'You think you're ready? You feel okay?' Glad asks as he helps me get dressed in a muted pink leather miniskirt I couldn't wait to show Sarah when she came home.

'Ready as snippers at bull-ball cuttin' time,' I say, borrowing Sarah's line. I put finishing touches on my makeup the way Sarah taught me. Glad makes me go light on the makeup, though. I want to take an iron and straighten out my hair so it flows like floss, but Glad won't hear of it.

'You really oughten not to be wearing any makeup. The natural look will make ya more lettuce than a face palette. Men pay for freckles and curls,' Glad says and wipes up my face with his hankie.

'Glad, you are a sight worse than a mother dressing her daughter for prom night,' Sundae laughs.

Sundae is a Texas honey-blonde with a bone bigger than Pie's. Sundae's specialty is cheerleaders. 'You'd be surprised by how many football players want a cheerleader with cock,' she says, adjusting the miniature pompoms in her hair.

Glad picked out a truck driver everyone knew.

'He's a nice man that only wants to diddle you,' Sundae says.

'Remember to watch the clock on the dash,' Pie says and gracefully kisses the air next to either side of my cheeks. 'Good luck.'

Glad just wrings his hands and makes me feel nervous.

I walk, in the flat white Mary Janes Glad made me wear instead of the spike heels I wanted, out of the caravans with everyone seeing me off, past The Doves, and into the lower-lit fluorescent nighttime of the overnight truck lot. The Nice Man's truck is right where Glad said it would be, five rows in and seven across. It is a plain truck, nothing special. No custom anything. The door is a dark blue and I can see my face mirrored in it. I squint my eyes so I can pretend I am seeing Sarah's reflection. I am supposed to tell the Nice Man my name is Cherry Vanilla, but after I knock and he says, 'Who is there?' the name 'Sarah' just comes out of my mouth.

At first I'm scared of the Nice Man. He reminds me of a New Orleans voodoo priest, his eyes rimmed with a thick black tattoo. Then I realize, after I sit on his lap a little and he talks to me in his near indecipherable Appalachian twang, that he is just a laid-off coal miner. And it's true what they say: the dust settles in every crease of skin like a new layer of pigment.

'Started in the mines when I was ten,' he says and places his charcoal-lined hands gently on my waist.

He is from Mingo County, West Virginia. Everyone in West Virginia, no matter how bad off they are, gives thanks at least they don't live in Mingo County.

'I used to lie in the bed with my brother at night while my mama listened to *The Christ Cure Radio Show* and my daddy sucked on a piece of coal to help his graveyard cough,' he tells me while bouncing me tenderly on his knee. I thought about asking him if he heard my grandfather's sermons too, as his show came on not too long after *The Christ Cure Radio Show* and was very popular in Mingo County, but I remember what Glad told me about not getting personal about my life.

'It ruins the fantasy of who they want you to be,' Glad had said.

'I do love Jesus,' the Nice Man says and begins to run his hands up under my pink skirt and to my peach panties. 'And you are such a sweet thing.' I hope he will say the name I told him. I want to hear her name while his hands begin to diddle me. I close my eyes and let him rock me and caress me.

'Sarah,' he finally whispers into my ear.

'I'm here,' I whisper back, 'not going nowhere.' I let my eyes roll back into my head in pleasure.

Sarah comes back a month after I've started working. The green-bean truck-driver man had stopped by to see her while she was gone. Other lizards were more than happy to be helpful and let him know Sarah's whereabouts. He was so mad that she was carrying on in some other state, with a cargo inspector at that, that he got rid of our room and put everything she'd left out on the brown lawn. Someone rang up Glad and I came and gathered up all the things and took them back to the caravan. Except her bubble bath. I left that sitting there on the rotting grass.

Mother Shapiro paid for Sarah to get our room back at the Hurley motel, but mostly Sarah stays with Mother in her caravan. They're always together. Sarah even starts acting like she cares about the lizards' moons too.

Mother Shapiro knows all the girls' monthly cycles by heart. At any given time, if Mother is sitting in The Doves, some lizard will holler out to her across the floor asking if they were ripe. Some want to know so they can force a driver they are fond of to settle down with them and a baby on the way. Some want to make sure they weren't gonna catch, so they can earn extra money risking sex without a rubber. Some just want to know so they can set aside enough money to get their feminine hygiene products ready. Mother Shapiro is pretty good at figuring out why a lizard wants to know. Folks say she has a second sight that way. Being a big believer in condoms, she usually yells back across

The Doves to the girl, 'Honey, you're as ripe to seed and as ready to take as a breeding sow!'

The only problem is most girls know that when Mother Shapiro overreacts like that she's just being protective and the coast is probably all in the clear.

Now Sarah acts like she knows the dates too, and discusses bleeding with Mother. I think about going up to Mother and telling her how many millions of times I've heard Sarah scream how she hates the 'plague.'

Mother Shapiro would invite me over to their booth to share a caramelized kiwi and walnut tart tatin when she sees me hovering nearby. Mother Shapiro asks me about how my dates are going and Sarah rolls her eyes away from me when I answer. Despite myself I try to interest Sarah in some good gossip from the World News newspaper.

'Said in the paper today that Elvis was really a hermaphrodite.'

'Read it already,' Sarah says and rolls her eyes again.

'Now, now . . .' Mother says. 'You two should really try to get along. You're family, aren't you?'

I realize by the way Sarah's eyes dilate that even Mother doesn't know exactly how we're related.

I slide out from the booth and before I walk away, I say with a small smile in a voice loud enough so those with good ears could hear, 'She's my mother.'

I hope Mother Shapiro will send for me, invite me to her trailer to snuggle under the goose-down blankets from Hungary with the two of them. Instead no one sees either one of them for weeks.

The candles in Mother's trailer blaze at night and Mother's broad outline can be seen lumbering past the drawn shades. It is said Sarah was taken with severe shock upon discovering she was my mother, and in public at that. All she could do was lie in bed and moan, while Mother Shapiro tended to her and tried to ply her with food.

Bolly tells me, 'She's got a freezer in there the size of a mare farm trough. I've been filling it for her with specials, in case a famine should hit.'

From outside their trailer I can smell reheated Appalachian foie gras with apple crisp in ver jus with grilled tender mango, and microwaved cider-cured spit-roasted pork loin with grilled figs and sweet Vidalia onion purée. Paxton is the only one who's set foot in there in two weeks, and that was very briefly. He brought them over a Tupperware of Osetra caviar dressing, which Mother had used her second sight to know Bolly had prepared.

'That place is lit in hundreds of beeswax candles,' Paxton said gravely. 'Your mother,' and I distinctly heard a tone of hostility directed at me as he said those words, 'is at death's doorknob.'

When I enter The Doves I notice an audible dip in the volume, which especially alarms me after reading that stuffed quail eggs braised in fresh huckleberries with English pea ravioli and miso-butter-poached chard is the day's special. Even a loud smash-up in the lot right outside The Doves wouldn't cause any notice to be taken when the menu was what it is today.

'Accusing someone of being your mother is a very serious thing,' Glad says to me sternly when I run back to the caravans in tears.

'Are they gonna play Davy Crockett for me?' I ask and put my head on Glad's lap.

'Oh no.' His hands slide through my curls. 'It just gonna take everyone a little time to get over it, that's all.'

I devote myself to proving I am not the inconsiderate scoundrel everyone thinks I am. I dedicate myself to being the best lot lizard ever, so one day I can walk into The Doves with the grandest-ever raccoon penis bone and make the place hush in awe and respect.

'On account of you being a greenhorn and two curves and a cuss fight away from entering your teenhood, it's best,' Glad says when I ask him why he's sending me out on only one or two dates a night.

All my john does is ohh and aww me, diddle me some, lick me like a lolly, and have me admire or laugh at the fuchsia French-cut underwear he has on under his worn-out jeans. I never get a chance to develop a second sight like Pie or Mother Shapiro. Glad always knows who they are and what they want down to a play-by-play. They never pay me either. That is all prearranged, down to my tip.

'I want to set the cab to rockin' and rollin' when I get in there, like a *real* lizard's trick would,' I complain to Glad. 'I want to stuff dollars into my shoes.'

'I'm not gonna let no one play with you,' he says and won't say any more on it.

'My penis bone is never gonna get bigger,' I complain to Sundae. 'I could make Glad a lot more money . . .'

'Well, Glad aspires to be a world-class pimp and to make the trucker's handbooks, but he also wants to be Santa Claus too. It is a hard combination for him. It makes him suffer terribly,' Sundae says mournfully.

I bow my head in deference to the contradictory proclivities of our pimp.

'Sometimes if you want more leash, you have to prove you can handle it . . .' Sundae mumbles while rolling over his anklet socks so they lie just so.

'What do you mean?' I squat down next to him.

'Well, you just gotta go after what you want,' Sundae says into his shin as he fluffs the lace on the sock. 'There is more than one truck stop around. There are a few drivers that will ride you over . . .' She presses a finger to her lips without looking at me.

'I won't say a word,' I say and smile.

My every other Thursday 7 p.m. gave me a ride up. After he put his Ben Davies black jeans on back over his ebony thong and lace-trimmed garter belt, I told him I had to see the Jackalope—the one with the antlers so big it is said fifty truckers can hang their caps on a point and there is still antler to spare.

'Why? You made me spit further than a llama,' he says buttoning up his red and black Coldmaster thermal long johns shirt over his Victoria's Secret Midnight Miracle Bra.

'I know,' I say and twirl a curl with my index finger the way I've seen Sarah do every time she asks for a man to make an honest woman out of her. 'But I feel my powers slipping some, and if they do, well, Glad might take me off the lot for . . .' I sigh like Sarah, 'For who knows how long until the malevolent drain on my magic disperses.'

'Malevolent, you say? That bad?' He shakes his head while lacing up his heavy steel-toe boots over his nylons, the seams running precisely up the back of his calves. 'Well, I agree. I think you need to pet the Jackalope to safeguard that sorcery you practice over every panty-wearing trucker in this hemisphere.'

He drives me over the Cheat, which I know Glad will never cross to get me.

'Too much evil sortilege,' Glad always says when someone suggests he open a franchise over Cheat Ridge. 'Many a man's been defrauded from his life by those mountains and river.'

He wouldn't even let one of his whores, even one who has completely lost his or her divinity, cross the Cheat for a pilgrimage to be restored by the patron saint of lot lizards: Holy Jack's Jackalope.

As soon as we pull into the gravel lot of the Holy we get slammed with the lingering scent of all the lizards' French colognes and perfumes, so strong it even masks the putrid scent of the bar's coal still behind back.

'Well, I'm going to drink a fair number of bourbon branches while you do your supplication,' he says. He checks his stocking seams under his cuffs and leaves for the dim insides of the quarry stone bar.

I walk around the side to where I see a line that stretches out the door. The lizards stand in their evening finest, the most palpable pinks, Armageddon reds, and enigmatic blacks. I pause before they spot me, shine my Mary Janes on the backs of my white knee-highs, and hike up my plaid skirt some. I dig out my lipstick from the separate makeup compartment in the leather overnight pack Sundae leant me and do a swift retouch. I jostle my curls and get close enough for them to see me. Most look out of habit, give me the once-over, then turn away with a dismissive flick of their locks.

Sarah always says before she goes man shopping, 'I look so good when I enter this bar, I'll make all the bitches nervouser than long-tailed cats at a rocking chair convention.'

A few of the younger girls keep their gaze on me and even give embarrassed half-smiles. No one wants to be thought of as needing to be here on this line, needing to be healed by the Jackalope. Being a lot lizard is one thing; being a failed one is a travesty.

I notice many lizards wear thick, mirrored highway-patrol shades and Palestinian head shrouds over their Dolly Parton wigs.

I smile back too energetically, so only the last girl on the line doesn't flick her head away in superiority at my obvious relief. She nods at me when I get to the end of the line. I nod back. I lean out and peer into the gloomy light of the bar. I can make out what looks like the spotlit tips of a white-striped antler, its huge points spreading out and up like the arms of Jesus.

'Good Lord, these hoes are taking their sweet time,' the girl in front of me mutters without looking at me. 'Been an hour near past and this line hardly moved. You'd think that Jackalope was paying these hoes by the minute!'

I notice her left eye behind her Hollywood sunglasses is half shut in black-and-blue lumps hardly concealed by streaks of powdery beige foundation.

'The trick is to use an oil-based, yellow-tone foundation. You should never use matte!' Sarah would say, wincing while tentatively sponging on tan goop. 'I swear it should say so on the bottle: "Do not under any circumstance use matte to cover your man's fist kisses."'

The girl notices me staring at her bruise and taps it like a lucky charm. 'My bell got rung . . .' She laughs coarsely.

I nod again. A few of the other lizards turn to us and scowl. No one else is talking, not even smoking. Just silently waiting in line like doughnuts on a conveyer belt waiting for filling.

'I gotta make more . . .' she says and swishes her mouth nervously back and forth as if she was getting ready to spit Listerine.

I want to tell her I'm well on my way to being one of Glading Grateful ETC . . .'s, of the world-renowned Doves, top moneymakers. And I want all the lizards on the line to overhear it too. I want them to know I don't need to see the Jackalope and that I don't even belong in this line. I'm an interloper, if the truth be known. I'm just hoping to speed up the process of earning one of the biggest raccoon penis bones ever.

'I know what you mean,' is what I say in a whisper so she'll whisper back.

She smiles with her lips turned down and reaches out her

hand. 'Pooh. Not like shit. Like Pooh-Bear.' The lizards turn toward us again. A few shush us.

'Hi, Pooh,' I whisper. 'I'm Sar . . .' I start, but remember I am trying to conceal my identity and don't want Glad to be able to track me down. 'Rrr,' I mumble and try to think of a name.

'Cool! Hi, She-Ra!' She shakes my hand again. 'She-Ra: Princess of Power was my favourite cartoon!'

'Would you please?!' a goodbuddy lizard dressed like a waiter in leather pants hisses out to us.

Pooh rolls her eyes and leans into my ear. 'I even had the She-Ra action figure.'

'She-Ra?'

She nods rapidly. The line takes little steps forward.

'Where you work at, She-Ra?' she whispers.

'Uh, around,' I whisper back.

She gives her glasses a shove up her nose bridge, which is so short the shades just slide back down again.

'I work at Three Crutches.' Her eyebrows go up above her glasses like fast little winks and she tilts her head at me expectantly. I nod.

'You ain't heard of Three Crutches?' she says incredulously under her breath. I shrug. 'Well, it's only the roughest, toughest truck stop in all of West Virginia.'

'Oh. Sorry.' I wince in sympathy for what horrors she probably has had to endure.

'I guess you ain't heard of Le Loup either?'

'Uh-uh.'

She leans in and cups my ear with her hand and says into it, 'He's the roughest, toughest pimp in all of West Virginia.' Her breath smells faintly like rubbing alcohol. 'And he's my man.' She steps back and regards me cautiously, as if I'll be so impressed, I just might spontaneously explode. I want to tell her about Glad.

I cup my hand and place it around her ear that's covered with so many silver rings all the way around it looks like a shower curtain holder. 'Do you want to get away from him?' I whisper.

She steps back again, pushes on her glasses and shakes her head. 'Are you nuts?' she says too loud.

'Some whores have no fucking respect,' one of the Palestinian Dolly Wigs mutters.

'I am his bestest and mostest and he loves me!' Pooh mutters to me. 'He took me in and made me everything I am!' She turns her back to me.

We say nothing, just take baby steps as the line painfully crawls toward the gaping stone doorway.

The woods are creaking with little snaps and rustles around us, the way woods do at the start of spring. The faint chugging of the still blends in with the steady hum of the grunts, hoots, and hollering of the truckers and pimps inside. More lizards stand in line behind me and I feel proud of myself for resisting the urge to glance at them. Pooh turns as each new one approaches and I hope she notices I'm not turning. Her eyes skip over me like I've evaporated. I notice she is smiling at the new lizards, but I can tell by the defeated way she turns back to face forward none of them has returned her smile, which gives me a righteous feeling of vindication.

Suddenly a shot goes off in the bar followed by the sound of a bottle smashing, and all the lizards stiffen with anticipation. They all watch the bar side to see if their pimp is coming raging out to grab them off the line like an angry parent pulling his kid from the playground. But the gruff bellow of 'Gentlemen, it was just an inadvertent discharge' calms the shouts in the bar and the line relaxes.

I stare up at the light coming down in shafts like long carrot stalks through the dogwood trees. By accident I lose my footing and step hard on the foot of the lizard behind me.

'Christ help me for I have sinned,' she says when I turn around to apologize. Her eyes are turned up so only the whites are showing and her blue lacquered lids quiver around them like a Jell-O mold. Her fingers are spread apart and tensed.

'Oh, shit!' Pooh laughs. 'Now you look like her! Can you look any more spooked?!'

I laugh, but it's out of relief that Pooh's talking to me again, so it's a little overdone and she eyes me suspiciously.

'We're almost there,' I say and point to the entrance of the Holy Jackalope shrine.

She turns toward it. 'About time too. When I heard that gunshot, I was for certain Le Loup would snatch me off this line before the sheriff showed. And I'll be John Browned if we actually make it in there.' I feel a surge of tenderness that she's included me, which dissolves into an irritating pathetic awareness at how lonesome I felt when she ignored me.

'Is your hair that color and curl nature-wise?' Pooh asks and waves a hand through my hair, then casually jerks out half a handful of her short bleached-platinum shag and flings it to the ground. 'I'm always jealous of girls that have albino hair.'

She catches me looking at her head. She makes a distracting noise like an orangutan and fluffs her hair so the bald patches are camouflaged.

I clear my throat in a friendly chimp kind of way and tell her, 'I'm not an albino. At least I don't think I am.' It doesn't occur to me to mention I'm not really a girl.

Suddenly we get blasted by a hail of spitball shushes from the lizards around us. Pooh uses her line-placement superiority to glare at the lizards queued behind us. Some of them cluck their tongues and suck their teeth. One of them says, 'You better watch it, *missies,*' which gives me an emery-board chill that isn't exactly unpleasant.

We move forward in line silently. Pooh turns to me now and then and mimics a lizard's face in various sordid sex acts: the 'choking on a pork bone' face, the 'sat on lickin' butt' face, and the ever-popular 'drunk trucker penis in the ear' face. That one makes me laugh out loud when I recognize it. I turn my face down expecting to be chastised, but I hear Pooh say JesusFuck-ShitFuck, and other lizards around us murmuring the same in reverent tones so I look up and I see the glowing aura of the Jackalope from inside the bar not six feet in front of us and I say it too, 'JesusFuckShitFuck.'

Pooh steps inside the stone entrance and I nearly smash my face following her.

I've heard it said many bars have tried to copy Holy Jack's by mounting up and doing dramatic lighting on a Jackalope. But just 'cause a bug squashed on a windshield looks like the Virgin Mary don't mean it's gonna be turnin' no bitters into brandy.

I've heard it said the barkeep at Holy Jack's had done some school way up North and he was just applying the crafty trickery you can't help but acquire being up North, but I saw no hidden spotlights hanging from the pine rafters. No hot-air vents or red coils either. Besides the candles all the lizards light and burn at its base, I saw nothing preternatural to account for the unearthly glow and intense heat radiating down on us from the Holy Jack-alope. It's so bright that those wearing shades don't even notice to take them off.

Mine and Pooh's mouths hang as we make our way into the small side room, past the lizards sobbing, filing out through to the bar.

I've heard it said too that women have brought their husbands that won't quit drinking their hairspray and nail-polish remover.

Mommas have brought their strip-mine babies born with arms growing out of their heads like rabbit ear antennas. Grandparents have brought their grandchildren blinded from masturbating. Not one of them was ever cured.

It's been said that it was Highway Patrol that hit and killed this Jackalope and a pack of renegade lot lizards held the wild run-over beast in their arms, cradling its bleeding head next to their exposed bosoms, warming its paws under their skirts and in their privates, and sucking on its once-tiny antlers with their painted mouths. And when the Jackalope passed, the lizards not only had the first real orgasms of their lives, but they suddenly were transformed into the most desired lot lizards at any truck stop ever. How that run-over Jackalope made its way here is a great mystery, but its charm for down-and-out trucker hoes spread to every lot lizard the world over.

I have to shield my eyes against its glow, but slowly I take it in. Caught in mid leap it lunges out, all four and a half feet of it. Steel brackets support it and bolt it to the wall. Every down-and-out pimp has made an attempt to steal this Jackalope. That's why a true-life Pinkerton guard sits off to the side, scowling.

The Jackalope has the most beatific smile on its face, and clouded eyes the color of wasabi. Its lush silver-brown fur looks so forgiving and noble, every lizard in the room cannot help but reach out to it sumptuously.

But what everyone is astounded by, including the cast and crew from the national TV news show that filmed here and is well documented by framed autographed photos which the Pinkerton also must guard, are the antlers. Apparently they keep growing. I've heard it said the roof has had to be raised five times just to accommodate the miracle. I can even make out the phosphorescent buds of new antler.

The smoky sanctified air combines with various evaporated

alcohols laced with moonshine's embalming fluids and causes actual storm clouds to form around the uppermost antlers. So as Pooh and I are glugging our mouths like fish do, it suddenly starts to rain pure tiger's sweat moonshine down from one of the antler clouds onto our tongues.

'Ah, yum yum.' Pooh licks her lips and opens her mouth wider to catch as much of the consecrated whiskey rainfall as she can. What drips into my mouth burns like lye so I spit it out, as respectfully as I can.

'I feel the Jackalope's power. Don't you, She-Ra?' Pooh moans.

I nod my head in slow motion. 'I do indeed, Pooh.' I realize my arms are stretched upward just like Pooh's and just like every other lizard's.

What I feel is a slow hard wave of silky insinuating electrical currents that makes every other lizard and me wave like at a revivalist meeting.

Some weep, some whimper. Everyone, even the male lizards, toss the last pair of underwear they wore on a trick into the offering barrel. I've heard it said that those undergarments make for a brisk mail-order business and finance the antler roof-raisings.

Soon a quiet Chinese gong sounds and the Pinkerton, without moving a muscle, says, 'Okay, ladies and gentlemen, you have five more minutes, then you need to take it into the bar. Thank you.'

Everyone closes their eyes tight and makes their prayer. I reach up under my blouse and grab my raccoon penis bone and clutch it tight. I chant to myself, 'Please, oh divine Jackalope, I want to be a real lizard. I want to *earn* a huge bone.' I open my eyes and stare up into its dead murky eyes. 'Make me a better lizard than Sarah,' I say with a force that invigorates and frightens me at the same time.

The gong sounds again gently and the Pinkerton clears his throat and the lizards start to progress toward the bar to toast their newfound libidinous powers.

Some old-timers put *Jake Leg Blues* by Daddy Stovepipe and Mississippi Sarah on the jukebox to make fun of some of the lizards that are temporarily paralyzed by the force of the Jackalope and now are walking like they drank bad moonshine.

All the pimps who are still able to see straight stumble over to their lizards to peruse their new improved commodities. I glimpse my every other Thursday 7 p.m. who drove me over here, slumped down in a corner with drool hanging down like an icicle.

'Le Loup!' Pooh shouts and she is engulfed into the open flaps of Le Loup's long leather coat like a little rodent snatched up by a bat. He lifts her small body and tosses her into the air before setting her back down.

'It was fantastic!' She claps her hands.

Le Loup only nods. Pooh motions me forward. I walk toward them, feeling my new fresh abilities surging through me.

'Oh, I'm gonna not disappoint you no more. I swear on it. I'm changed, changed, changed. It's done!' Pooh has tears in her eyes. 'No more dates gonna complain about me ever again.'

I move next to her. 'Oh, Le Loup, this is She-Ra. She-Ra, Le Loup.' She gently touches her bruised eye.

I look up into the fuzziest face I have every seen. Long black bushy sideburns take up most of his face. His eyes peering over his facial shrubbery are so small and dark I think they must just be the raisin eyes stolen off a gingerbread man's face.

He nods and runs his hand through his slicked-back oiled hair, then takes my hand in his. 'Pleased to meet you, Miss She-Ra.' He bends down and kisses my hand. His hand feels damp and smooth like the exposed under-part on a just-fixed dog. He gives me a big smile with no teeth. As we walk through the bar, I spy him taking me in. He gives me a gentlemanly wag of his head in approval and I feel myself flush with pleasure.

'Aw, and you blush too,' he says and squats down so his head is at my chest.

'I blush too!' Pooh says eagerly. 'I mean, if I'm embarrassed I will, I guess nothing's done been doing me that for some time, but I think—'

'Shhh!' Le Loup makes us both jump. 'Sorry, honey, did I scare you?' he says and caresses my hand. 'Just your friend Pooh there has never learned when to quiet down.'

'Sorry, I'm sorry,' Pooh whispers. 'Sorry . . .'

Le Loup never takes his gaze away from me.

'So pretty,' he says and I feel myself flush again. 'I love your Goldilocks curls . . . Who you here with, honey?'

I point to every other Thursday 7 p.m. folded over in the corner.

'Oh, well, he looks like he's hangin' in there like a hair on biscuit.' He laughs, Pooh laughs, I laugh.

'He ya daddy?' he says through his smile.

I shake my head.

'You work for him?'

I shake my head. He smiles wider.

'Who you work for?' he says into my neck. His breath smells like licorice.

I shrug.

'Precious little princess you are . . .' He laughs, Pooh laughs, I laugh. I notice the seams on the shoulders of his leather are coming apart.

'Look at me playing twenty questions with you and you must be starving, waiting on that line hours!' He lets go of my hand and stands.

Pooh rubs her stomach. 'I sure would love a hillbilly pop and a big chicken-fried steak because I am—'

Le Loup shoots her a fast look. He reaches down his hand for my hand and I take it. I let him escort me into the dining room.

'Starving . . .' Pooh mutters behind us.

'Aren't you precious,' Le Loup says after I carefully cut the burnt black gristle off the half of chicken-fried steak I'm splitting with Pooh.

I want to tell them about Doves Diner and Bolly and the big French white puffy chef's hat he earned. I want to take out my bone, dangle it before their eyes and tell them I'm going to earn the grandest one ever. But I say nothing.

Le Loup tosses boiled peanuts into the air and I swear I can see his tongue unfurl like an iguana's and pluck them out of midair.

'Want some West Virginia spring water?' Pooh starts to pour me some of the clear liquid out of a jam-jelly glass.

'Don't you get her on that rotgut!' Le Loup swipes at her hand.

'Sorry . . .' Pooh takes a big swig and coughs.

'So, as I was saying . . .' His hand strokes my hair and I can't help but lean into his touch. 'If you come work for me'—his finger grazes the tip of my ear, raising the hairs on the back of my neck—'you'll have a million Barbie dolls. You like Barbie? How many Barbies have I got you, Pooh?'

'A lot,' Pooh says and spits after making sure Le Loup isn't looking at her.

'I'd get you all the outfits. Just got Pooh the loveliest fur coat made just for Barbie.'

Pooh pushes her eyes farther back into her head.

I nod.

'You'll want for nothing ever.' His fingers wiggle under my chin, tickling me so I involuntarily jerk my chin to my chest, catching his hand there. He leaves it. Then slides it inside my blouse and over my heart.

'I'm the best daddy you'll ever have,' he says in a low voice that's half whisper, half growl.

I look down to watch his hand rising and falling with my breath. I close my eyes. The warmth of his hand penetrates me. Le Loup lets out a laugh and presses harder on my heart.

I snap my eyes open to see his face breaking into an immense smile, this time with teeth.

Boxcutter teeth with gold trim impressed with Norse warrior designs.

'Welcome aboard!' He laughs.

We pile into Le Loup's purple Trans Am. Pooh climbs over me to sit next to Le Loup. We speed through winding back-roads that make the tires screech and produce thick billows of red dust. I take little sips of the clear liquid in Pooh's jam-jelly jar and it burns my throat like a thousand fire-ant bites. My eyes get too heavy to keep open as the orange reflector lights and the yellow eyes of deer and mountain cougar blaze by us. I start to lean on Pooh, my head falling on her shoulder. With a firm shove, she pushes me, redirecting me to sleep against the door.

'It's gonna rain down hard . . .' Pooh says.

I slowly let my eyes focus on the substantial stone masonry of the Vatican.

'You best get up, 'cause Le Loup just laid a black snake belly-up on the freeway divider.'

Pope John Paul II's face is in the middle of the Vatican, set agreeably upon a bed of curlicue fuchsia hearts.

'Sky sure looks bluer than end-of-the-month balls though,' Pooh says.

When I rock my head back and forth, Pope John Paul II winks at me and seems to pucker out little kissies.

'A black snake, belly-up, is sure to make it wet as a lizard's poing after pay day,' Pooh says.

I try respectfully to blow a kiss back to Pope John Paul II, but my mouth only flaps.

'You can't hold your liquor.' Pooh's face appears over me, blocking out Pope John Paul II and the Vatican. I try to look past her.

'You heaved up pretty good.' Pooh smiles, then suddenly barks a loud laugh showing a mouth full of fuzzy gray teeth. Her bruised face appears to liquefy and undulate like goulash. 'How you managed to splatter all over a car interior and not catch a speck on your own self must be an act of the Lord.' She barks again. 'Not a speck . . . but your breath . . .' She waves her hand in front of her face. 'Panther's breath!' Pooh motions to the poster on the ceiling above us. 'Le Loup even laid you out under His Holiness. You was gonna have your baptism, but he got a whiff . . .' Pooh waves her hands again and makes a sourball face. 'Le Loup is a devout Catholic, you know. He anoints all his girls here. He would've put out the consecrated satin zebra sheets, but I said you might blow again, so he laid out a garbage bag under you instead.' Pooh bays again.

I roll my head to the side and have a hard time noticing when it stops.

'I doubt he'll put you out without getting you first.' Pooh climbs off me. I slowly look around the room. Everything is furry.

'But 'cause of the snake, it is gonna storm, and when it storms, all them truckers stuck in their cabs . . . we're gonna be busy!'

Everything in the small room is covered in fur. Thick, matted brown bear fur. The couch, the coffee table, there's even fur wainscoting.

'I imagine he wants to test the Jackalope in us, and that's why he put out the black snake . . .'

She sits on the fur couch and grabs a small jam-jelly jar off the fur coffee table. She blows across the clear liquid in the glass but no steam puffs, then she gulps it all down in three quick swallows. 'It's gonna pour,' she says, leaning over and moving aside the window shade. 'Gotta fortify.'

I nod.

'You'll learn how. You want some breakfast?' Before I can answer, she's pulling my arm, making me sit up. She suddenly pushes back my chin so I'm being winked at by Pope John Paul II again. 'He didn't even bite ya!' She gives my chin a subtle shove back down. 'Well, he will.' She grins again. 'Faster than a fart in a whirlwind, he'll take you.'

I'm not sure how to respond to the half-conscious acrid friendliness in her eyes, so I retch.

'Ewww, God!' She hops off the bed. 'You trash Le Loup's car, now you want to do me again? And don't think he won't make you pay for that, precious!'

'Sorry,' I say and try to find her eyes under the swelling.

She shakes her head and grabs her glass and shakes out a drop into her mouth.

'I'm supposed to get you breakfast. So let's go.'

I pull myself off the bed and peel away the garbage bag stuck to my legs.

'I have to . . .'

'One is the closet, the other is the crapper. I'll let you be adventurous.'

I can't see my feet in the deep fur as I walk over to the two doors. I open one and its insides are pitch-black and filled with cricket noises. I slam that one shut and open the other.

It smells like an elephant, so I wade through the thicker fur till I find a wooden slat commode next to a cracked full-length mirror.

I stare at myself in the mirror. My curls are a little fuzzy, but that is the appropriate outcome for not taking Sundae's advice to apply an overlay of prime-coat VO5. Pooh is right, though; no vomit got me. And aside from my plaid skirt and cotton blouse being a little wrinkled and my kneesocks rolled down, I am disappointed to see I look almost the same as I did when I left The Doves.

Pooh grabs my arm as I come out of the bathroom. 'I gotta get you fed, so let's go.' She pulls me out of the converted barn, slamming and locking up the wide wood barn doors behind us.

'Ugh, never get used to the stink of swamp lantern roses!' Pooh holds her nose and points to the yellow flowers blooming out of the skunk cabbages lining the marsh like rows of hepatitis eyeballs.

We walk past trailers rusted in not unpleasant mauve and copper shades and broken-down tin shacks with red velvet curtains till we get to the truck lot. Eighteen-wheelers are precariously balanced on hugely broken-up disjointed tar slabs that surround, like petals on a daisy, a dilapidated diner truck stop. On its summit is a magenta neon sign of three crutches joined up like the musketeers' swords.

'Three Crutches,' Pooh says. 'Founded by three beat-up lot lizards.' She suddenly presses her hand under my eyes. 'You ain't got the crutches' stigmata yet?'

I move my face away and then it hits me. Tears well up into my eyes.

'Ahh, there they are!' Pooh laughs.

I squat down on the ground and hold my eyes burning so intensely I can't open them to see. 'I can't see, Pooh!'

Pooh laughs.

'My eyes, Pooh, my eyes!' I rub them violently, trying to get rid of the fierce throbbing.

She laughs again, grabs under my arms, and drags me up. 'Let's go, Shirley Temple. I got no time to play. I'm supposed to feed you.'

'I can't see!' I cry as I stumble. 'I'm blind, Pooh, please!'

'Welcome to Three Crutches, baby doll! Now let's go.' She yanks me forward.

I walk, clutching Pooh with my left hand while flailing at my dripping eyes with my right. 'Up, up . . .' Pooh says as my feet hit stairs and she pulls me up from a topple.

Then it hits me harder. A horrendous acrid odor engulfs us. All sorts of issue start running out of my nose.

The sound of aluminum steps echo under my feet. I'm grasping for a rail to hold but find none and end up clasping Pooh with both arms. 'Please help me, Pooh, I'm blind!' I sob.

'Quit your whining. You wanted to come here, didn't you? You asked for this!' She lurches me up a few more steps. 'Playing all cutesy with Le Loup!' I hear the jingle of bells on a door and the warmth of inside hits my wet face.

'I can't see!' I cry in a panic, hoping someone will take pity and call a doctor and save me. 'I can't see! And my face is melting!'

'Pooh, you're worse than a boy with a box of matches and a stray cat!' a woman's husky voice calls out. 'I know Le Loup wouldn't like to know you'd be torturing his greenhorn, now would he?'

'I didn't do anything, Stella!' Pooh spits.

'Give her here . . .' Pooh releases me into someone's arms. I am instantly hoisted backward onto her lap like an amusement park ride that lifts you with G force.

'Hand me the spray bottle, Lymon!' Her limbs are so bony and protruding and her scent has a damp muddiness to it, it feels as if I'm cradled in a twig nest. I desperately rub my eyes.

'Hi, honey. I'm Stella and Pooh's just toying with you some. Bad Pooh, bad . . . Here ya go . . .' A fine jasmine-perfumed mist coats my face. 'Open your eyes, open . . .' She pulls my lids up and I feel the tiny mist droplets hit my eyes and immediately soothe them.

'Pooh didn't give you no lemon wedge, did she?' Stella sucks her tongue. 'Tsk, tsk.'

I begin to blink, my eyes sopping up the sweet spray like graham crackers in milk. 'Pooh!' she scolds again. 'Here . . .' She slips something so sour under my upper lip that my mouth curdles. I try to spit it out. 'Uh-uh . . . keep it in . . . it's a lemon wedge and if you want to see again you best keep it in.' She puts her earthy-smelling hand over my mouth.

'Here now, close up your eyes and let them heal up.' She presses my lids down and runs her hands over the jasmine mist coating my face like a fine sweat. 'Pooh's just afraid you've got a sweeter tang than she does, but no one has a sweeter tang than Pooh, ain't that right, Pooh?' I hear laughter around us.

'Don't pee down my back and tell me it's raining!' Pooh yells. 'Y'all just too bored and forlorn! Well, I'm not! I got things to get done!' Pooh stomps away down the aluminum stairs.

'Pickled tang is more likely,' someone calls out.

'I would be worried if I were Pooh,' a high-pitched man's voice says. 'I'd like a taste on ya . . .' I feel fingers in my hair that carry on them a whiff of the biting odor that makes my eyes well up again.

'Lymon! Get back in the kitchen. She ain't even got her

bite marks and you're ready to take a piece of her?! I should tell
Le Loup! Now get!' Stella motions so hard with her arms shooing
Lymon away, she dumps me out of her lap. I hit the floor with a
thud and the lemon wedge shoots out of my mouth like a bullet.
I open my eyes and through a haze see the wedge fly into the face
of a raptor that sits on the windowsill.

'Oh, damn . . . dropped my lap baby . . . shoot.' Everyone
laughs until the stunned raptor starts flapping its wings and caw-
ing like a sat-on cat. Then everyone rushes to soothe it, making
barnyard animal sounds to remind the insulted raptor of its favor-
ite prey and put it in a good mood.

And suddenly I start to cry. Not from the fiery smell that
makes me want to rip my eyeballs out of my head. Not from
being dropped with a thud and hearing a roomful of people I
could barely see laugh and then ignore me for a raptor. I cry deep
disconsolate wails from suddenly missing Sarah, even if she often
forgot she was my momma.

'Oh, I hope I ain't broke ya. Le Loup would just kill me if I
broke ya brand-new! Did I break ya?' Stella's twiggy fingers lift
and twist my limbs like I'm a rag doll.

I try to tell her I'm not broken, but when I open my mouth all
that comes out is, 'Sarah, Sarah, Sarah.'

'Sarah, that your name? That's a sweet name. Maybe you'll
be like Sarah in the Bible, and the Lord will knock you up when
your tang is as leathery as a sow's purse.' Stella pats my head.

'The Lord can give the curse of life to the most unlikely
being,' says another woman.

'That's why I didn't even bother having my tubes done in!
I just know Jesus will make an example out of me, just like he
done Sarah,' Stella says and pats my head again.

'Now why would he impregnate you? I never miss services
and my vagina is as dry as a well dug in the Sahara! Plus the

Lord knows I would not laugh at him finding myself pregnant like our friend Sarah here did.' The woman leans over and pats my shoulder.

'I've never been pregnant before,' I say between sobs.

'Well, you know, you can't get lard unless you boil the hog.'

'I had my triplets using five layers of rubbers with a layer of tin-foil gum wrapper thrown in for good measure . . .' says a woman so narrow and white she looks like a body-of-Christ wafer. 'So why isn't that just the same as what did Sarah here?' She pats my neck.

'I don't believe I was ever pregnant . . .' I wipe at my face.

'Well, Mary Grace, did the Lord tell you what he was gonna do to you?'

'Did you hear *Him*?' Lymon yells as the raptor swooshes and dive bombs over our heads.

'I could've been with baby and didn't even know.' I blink some tears back and press my hands into the hollow barren feeling I'm used to in my gut.

'Well, I thought one night I heard *Him* when I was with my babies still in,' Mary Grace says. 'My stomach was moving and heaving and voices were coming from my person, but it turned out just to be gas.'

'Mary Grace, you just got hit with very acidic ejaculit,' says another woman. 'I heard of truckers' juice so full of strip-mine slag they can burn through a wooden condom!'

'That can produce very unsettling gas,' Lymon agrees.

'I know I've felt the movements inside me sometimes,' I whisper, remembering those times when one of Sarah's boyfriends would come at me when she was out late working. They'd kick over empties in the dark, pull back my blankets, and move into me, taking me over with silent invasive thrusts. I liked the ones that lay with me after, held me so tight to them with hands that could easily break me in two but didn't. They'd stroke my stomach and whisper in my ear, 'Sweet baby, sweet baby, I'm inside ya baby.' I also remember the blood after, after they take it all out of me. It felt like they must of pulled out the sweet baby and all my innards. Then they'd take it away with them.

I make a fist and punch at the loss inside myself.

'Why're you hitting at yourself?' Mary Grace says and slaps my hands down. 'Don't do that. Here, have a lemon wedge.' Mary Grace slips a sour slice under my lip.

I suck on the lemon and let the bitterness wash everything down my throat.

'Hey now.' Mary Grace pats my head. 'Your eyes better yet?'

I nod.

'Let's get you off that floor.' Stella picks me up under my arms. 'You're gonna have to keep that lemon wedge in your mouth until you've eaten here enough so you're immune.'

I nod again.

'Best to remember to take it out before oral sex though. Most of these truckers drive varnishing the flagpole, one hand on each of their sticks, steering with their knees, so by the time they get to you, it's damn near whittled down to a toothpick, covered in blisters and sores. When Pooh started here she gave so many men lemon head the infirmary was filled with men with concussions from hittin' their heads on the cabs' roofs.' Stella cradles me up in her bony, bruised-up arms.

'You'll get used to the taste before your face gets frozen in that expression,' Mary Grace says, floating by.

'I'm gonna start your immunity now. Lymon, bring us out a big plate of livermush fry topped with red-eye gravy, a slab of fatback with some sorghum syrup, and hoe cakes to sop it all up,' Stella calls out as she carries me into the dining room. 'And of course a whole mess of ramps!'

'Ramps . . .' everyone mutters and half chuckles.

'Do you think Le Loup wants her on the ramps?' another girl says. 'He might be designing to advertise her as one girl without the ramp flatulence. Be an awful big draw . . .'

'Well, Petunia, that might well be,' Stella says while moving us into a ripped-up Day-Glo-orange dining booth. 'But if she does not partake of the ramps, she's gonna be fart-free sucking on stick shift 'stead of the weasel, she'll be so blind! I know our boys rather have a tube-steak shine than a deodorized whore. If that ain't the truth, you'd have no business.'

Stella pulls out a bunch of napkins from the dispenser and mops up what's left of my tears off my face.

'The more ramps you eat, the more you won't be bothered by them,' Stella says, blowing my nose for me.

I nod.

'You never had ramps?' Petunia asks incredulously.

I nod no.

'You ain't a West Virginian girl, then,' Stella laughs. 'Ramps is like onions . . .'

'Only a hundred times stronger!' Petunia says.

'Lymon picks 'em wild and we have big old ramp feeds,' Stella says, pouring out handfuls of salt and tossing it over her shoulder.

'But them ramps, when they're getting cut, before they hit the bacon fat, mercy me! They burn like the clap, that is if you got the clap in your eyes, which I heard told can occur on occasion,' Petunia says.

'So you gotta eat the ramps, then the stink of the raw ones won't bother you. You'll be immune. Poor little girl never had ramps . . .' Stella tsk-tsks.

'Oh,' I say. I want to tell them about Bolly at The Doves and the fine French shallots he sautés in a delicate saffron-infused lobster-chocolate-reduction sauce, but I say nothing.

'Here ya be . . .' Lymon says, and puts in front of us three steaming plates on the oilcloth table cover. My eyes start watering again. Before I can even get my hand up to rub them, Lymon is spraying my face with the soothing mist while Stella pulls out the lemon from under my lip and forks a shovelful of ramps into my mouth. I chew the greasy, pungent onions and blink up the spray.

'Gonna send you back with a spray bottle of your own. How you like them ramps?' Stella says through a mouthful.

I nod and reminisce about Bolly's sweet-onion mint pesto served on house-cured sturgeon.

'And for dessert you can have tomato and ramp sorbet with mayonnaise crème!'

'I even have pawpaw cookies!' Lymon whispers into my ear, his tongue reaching into the inside of my Eustachian tube. He blasts my face fast with spray to preempt the tears from his ramp juice musk.

Stella keeps feeding herself and me. I'm chewing and swallowing as fast as I can, but she's picking up speed, till finally I keep my mouth closed and she stabs my lips with her fork.

'Mmmm!' I cry while keeping my mouth sealed.

'Ooh, sorry, sorry . . . are ya bleeding? Oh, just a bit, here . . .' Stella shoves napkins at my mouth.

'Le Loup is gonna ask why his new girl's mouth sprays out cum like a watering can and I'm gonna tell him he's got Stella to thank for the extra holes!'

'Petunia, you're 'bout to lose the remainder of those teeth . . . though I would be doing you a boon to your fellating capacity.'

'Humpf!' Petunia says.

'You stopped your bleeding, Sarah?' Stella takes the napkin gag off my mouth. I nod yes and wipe at the cut. 'Did I overhear you say you had a baby?'

I clear my throat and say, 'I've had babies inside me, but I didn't think that could be. Just like Sarah in Genesis. My mom had the same thing happen to her it seems like.' They nod their heads.

'The Bible is very handy for teaching love and understanding of one's kin,' Stella says, nodding at Petunia.

'Did they take your baby to harvest body organs?' Petunia asks, showing a tongue full of gray liver-mush.

'I would bleed after,' I tell them and open my mouth for a bite of cornbread 'hoe cakes' that Stella's fingers are bringing to me.

'If you bled, then you can be assured it was a Yankee come and stole it with their sticky-as-crap-cooking-on-tar fingers. Your baby's innards are long sold off and the carcass tossed in some incinerator without a decent Christian burial!' Petunia shouts, launching bits of fatback into my face.

'But *my* mother didn't know she had me, and I don't think I had my innards taken by Yankees. They were truck drivers mostly,' I tell them.

'I bet they were just Yankees posing as truck drivers!' Petunia says.

'My mother whipped me if she saw the blood. She'd cry that I steal all her sweet babies from her,' I say, picturing my underwear with the little clots of scarlet I'd leave out for her to find, to feel that moment of importance before she reached for the strap.

'Oh, Petunia, this is so woeful,' Stella says. 'That's a travesty, your mama blaming you for those Yankee thieves stealing her granbabies and your innards.'

'I knew there was something missing from inside me,' I say.

I remember after some of the truck drivers left, and they always left, how Sarah would sit and wail while punching at her stomach.

'We have a real tragic figure on our hands here. We better

warn Le Loup that Sarah here might drop dead at any time so to be easy on her.'

'No, if we tell Le Loup that she is of precarious health, he might work her doubly hard, seeing as he would want to get his money's worth!'

'Who'd he buy you from?' Stella asks, scooping a big fork of ramps into my mouth.

'He didn't buy me. I met him at the Jackalope.'

'So he stole ya!' Petunia gasps. 'Well, no wonder he put a black snake belly-up on the freeway divider!'

'Why?' I say and savor a spoonful of surprisingly tasty tomato and ramp sorbet with mayonnaise crème that Lymon had silently placed on the table during our conversations.

'A black snake belly-up on a fence or freeway divider brings rain, no matter how blue the sky! Everybody knows that!' Just then a flash of lightning races through the diner, followed by an ominous thunderclap. 'And when it rains we all get busier than a one-armed paper hanger!'

'Le Loup wants to get as much out of you before your man comes to claim you back,' Petunia explains. 'No pimp would let a lizard as cute as a toe sack full of puppies, like you are, escape on them. Aha!' she exclaims, pressing her hands to her head as if she were having a migraine. 'You were seeing the Jackalope to try to recover from your recent tragedy of loss. And you were supplicating to the Jackalope that it might restore the elasticity to your after-birth vagina!'

'You could have worked with the sheriff's department as a psychic, Petunia,' Stella says. 'You're way better at deducing the truth than doing whoring!'

'I take great offense at that comment. I am a damned good lizard. I haven't even needed to see the Jackalope, unlike your weekly pilgrimages!'

'I have never been to see the Jackalope!' With that, Stella stands, sending me sliding off her lap, under the table, and landing on the floor with a thump.

As they fight across the table, food flying, swearing, Mary Grace squats under the table beside me.

'I'm sorry for all the grave adversity you've recently endured,' she says and reaches with her hands for me. We duck down to avoid the flying cutlery and head into the kitchen. Lymon sticks a lemon wedge coated with sugarcane under my lip and leaves his finger a little too long in my mouth, so Mary Grace jerks it out.

'Lymon!' Mary Grace slaps his hand.

'I wouldn't've thought she was old enough to bleed. She ain't knee-high to a duck,' Lymon says.

'I never ever had the monthly blood,' I say.

Everyone in the kitchen gasps.

'Never?' Mary Grace pats my hand. 'Are you sure?'

I nod. 'I've had a bleeding hemorrhoid that I had to take to wearing a menstrual pad for . . .'

'That's a different hole,' Mary Grace says gravely.

Everyone nods in agreement.

'Well, you heard what happened to Sarah in Genesis. The Lord does not need blood to make a female with child. Lord!' She caresses my face. 'You are not only a figure of tragedy but are a miracle in our midst.' She crosses herself and kisses my hand.

I feel a warmth spread through me, as if I were bending over the bed waiting for Sarah's strap to comfort me.

'Shit! Now Le Loup is gonna really charge more for a poke with you,' Lymon moans.

The dishwasher kneels before me and begins to kiss my Mary Janes and sing religious songs in Cajun.

'Maybe you are Sarah, Abraham's wife reincarnated, and this

time the Lord is starting you early so you don't have to be one hundred by the time your kid is ten,' says one of the ramp cutters.

I nod solemnly and picture the real Sarah back at The Doves. I feel a conspicuous ache of pleasure combined with shame that I am not sharing with her her probable rightful place as a religious icon, on account of her having lost her innards probably thousands of times and giving birth to me without knowing it.

'Le Loup won't know whether to fuck you or worship you!' Lymon says, and Mary Grace slaps him.

Stella and Petunia come bursting through the kitchen swing doors.

'Sarah here is in all probability and likelihoods Sarah from Genesis reincarnated,' Mary Grace tells them, crossing herself again.

After Mary Grace updates Stella and Petunia on my status as a religious icon and probable sainthood, Stella nods, while Petunia immediately slides on her knees to my feet like she's stealing a base. 'I just know the *World News* and even *The Enquirer* will be here any minute! They always know when there is a supernatural occurrence anywhere in the world. I heard they have a whole team of psychics devoted to keeping them abreast of miraculous developments.'

A big burst of lightning flashes, followed by a thunderclap that makes everyone jump.

'Normally, we would've lost all our power from a hit like that!' Lymon gasps.

'I didn't even see a flicker,' says a ramp cutter.

Everyone moans like self-flagellated monks, and they all drop to their knees before me.

'What y'all doin'?!' Pooh says, slamming the screen door behind her.

Nobody says a thing. I feel hands sliding over my Mary Janes and knee-highs like a den of diamondbacks.

'Hi, Pooh,' I say and give her a big detached smile.

'What the hell are all y'all doin'?!' Pooh stomps closer.

'We've got to tell Le Loup! Where is he at, Pooh?' whispers Mary Grace, not turning her head from me.

'Tell him what?' Pooh stomps closer.

'Why that Sarah here is a Biblical figure reincarnated!' proclaims Stella.

'Or maybe possessed,' says the ramp cutter and everyone shoots him evil looks. 'In a saintly sort of way, I mean.'

'What?!' Pooh stares at me and I look down in embarrassment. 'First she's She-Ra the action figure, now a goddamned saint?!' Pooh spits, everyone gasps, and three different people put their hands over my eyes, ears, and nose to protect me from the vileness spilling forth from Pooh. But I can still make out her words. 'You want to know where Le Loup is?! He's gettin' the insides of his Trans Am steam-cleaned from a tornado of puke She-Ra the saint over there blew, yet walked out of there clean as dog balls.'

'Ohh, I feel the presence!' wails the dishwasher removing his hands from my eyes. 'My hands are hotter'n the hubs of hell!'

Hands are removed from my ears and nose and blown on as if they were set afire.

'So, she spewed like a tornado in Le Loup's little Trans Am?' Stella says slowly to Pooh.

'Yep, that's what your fuckin' saint did, after guzzling my stumphole whisky, which I think y'all clearly been guzzling too!'

'And not a drop got on her?' Petunia says, her voice wavering.

'Yup, like a spoilt brat! She coated me pretty good, though!'

'Pooh, why didn't you tell us of this miracle?!' Mary Grace gasps.

'Hallelujah! Hallelujah! Hallelujah!' someone shouts.

'What the fuck are y'all even on about?' Pooh yells.

'We needed something like this,' Stella says, massaging my calves. 'This will put Three Crutches on the map!'

'Give that old Jackalope a run for its money!' Petunia whispers between licks of my shoes.

'You all look like a bunch of pickled crab apples down there. Okay, joke's over! You got me, ha-ha-ha! Okay, I got to get She-Ra back ready for Le Loup to baptize her, so if y'all kindly move aside there . . .'

'Stella, remember to remind Le Loup that there is no cause to baptize her. She's already a holy lizard,' Mary Grace says.

Pooh glares at me. 'She's a whore, okay, just a whore, just like all of you. Ain't nothin' holy about her, okay? She's gonna be digging for change on her back just like all of you come nightfall, so y'all just get over yourselves, okay?!' Pooh lunges for me.

'Oh, Sarah can't work like you can, Pooh,' Lymon says, holding her back while on his knees. 'She's missing her insides. The Lord can take her at any moment.'

Pooh's eyes scrunch up real tight at me. 'I knew there was something about you I didn't like. I saw it in your eyes.' She backs up toward the door. 'Something too hungry in your eyes. I think you're really a black snake and you got everyone charmed. Well, not me! And you can sure as bet Le Loup is not gonna fall for this bullshit spell.'

'Pooh, if she were really a black snake, how would she've made it past all the ash trees planted around this diner? You know ash trees protect against black snakes!' Stella says.

'Might could slip through, if she took on the body of a rattler first,' says the ramp cutter.

Everyone ignores him.

'I heard this wind blow before and y'all gone fuckin' nuts!

And you'—she points to me 'you'll pay for this. You'll pay.'
Pooh turns around and stomps out.

'Think like you're carrying tomato dumplings, y'all.' Stella directs the crowd from Three Crutches Diner as they gently hoist me up onto the soft pads of their fingertips to carry me back for some rest before the coming media onslaught.

'She's lighter than a fart,' the ramp cutter says.

'You would be too if you were a saint missing organs,' the dishwasher hisses.

Everyone shushes them and they carry me outside, down the aluminum stairs, and begin to sing *Must Jesus Bear the Cross Alone?* in the key of A.

'"Must Jesus bear the cross alone, And all the world go free?"' they sing.

I stare up at the gray clouds tumbling over one another like a circus act.

'"No, there's a cross for ev'ry one, And there's a cross for me . . ."'

It feels as if I'm floating on hundreds of Q-tip heads.

'"The consecrated cross I'll bear, Till death shall set me free . . ."'

The sweet ozone smell of rain and the low sky above me fill me with a gracious tenderness.

'"And then go home my crown to wear, for there's a crown for me."'

I let my arms fall to the side, outstretched like a T, the symbolism of which is not lost on the crowd carrying me, and they let out a loud moan of delectation.

'"O precious cross! O glorious crown! O resurrection day!"' they sing louder and I hum along.

'"Ye angels from the stars come down . . ."' Somebody stops holding my ass with their fingertips and instead cups it with their hands, giving it a gentle squeeze. '"And bear my soul away . . ."'

'Lymon!' someone shout-whispers, and I feel the hands slapped away from my bottom.

I close my eyes and just float. I imagine Sarah next to me. I reach out my hand to her and she lets me hold her hand.

'"One did give his life up for an unworthy soul such as I . . ."' they sing, and I hum along to Nailed to the Cross in the key of F.

I smile at my mom. She hates the romantic spirituals, but tends to enjoy the ones that contain great bodily harm to Jesus.

'Jesus is just like a trucker—takes a whore off her back,' she'd rave after some lizard would find Jesus. 'Convinces her he's the fuckin' Son of God and always fuckin' leaves her. How the fuck is she supposed to make her money after she's gotten used to sleeping on her side?!' she'd spit. 'Fucking Christ! Yeah, he'll never fill me more than trucker dollars. Give me the first fuckin' nail!'

'". . . All my sinning is purged. They are hammered to the cross, nailed to the crucifix . . ."' everyone sings.

'You're gonna pay,' Sarah says to me with her clouded smile, eyes glimmering like flakes of blue glaze.

'It's different this time,' I whisper.

'"He bore so much willingly, the anguish, the loss, He suffered with glee . . ."' they sing.

She pulls her hand from mine. 'You're still stealing what's mine,' she says, her mouth taking a sarcastic downturn. 'Like you always do and you always, always pay.' She winks at me and points up to the sky.

'"Jesus died on the cross. My sins He took with him there."'

I jerk open my eyes to see a turkey vulture circling unsteadily above us, its two-toned wings spread into a wobbly V. A fat rain-drop splatters against my forehead.

'It's fixin' to come up a bad cloud,' Lymon says and gives my ass a courteous fondle.

'It is way too early for spirituals!' Le Loup's deep resinous voice booms over us, interrupting *Beneath the Crucifix of Jesus* in the key of D flat. 'And why are you carrying my new baby like you're putting on a Sunday school Easter show?'

I lift my head to see Le Loup standing in his barn doorway, Pooh peeking out from behind him, laughing.

Stella stomps up to Le Loup and talks to him fervently, point-ing at me occasionally. Pooh rolls her eyes, laughs, and spits. Le Loup narrows his small eyes at me. I try to look virginal by making my eyes look big.

When Sarah was after someone else's man, she'd put her hair into pigtails and practice making her eyes wide in the mirror. 'Nothin' makes a man want you more than thinking you're an unpopped virgin. This make the best virgin blood,' she'd say, slip-ping a Burger King foil ketchup packet into her bra. 'Makes them feel like fuckin' God.'

'Well put our little angel down!' Le Loup motions to the group like he's guiding in an eighteen-wheeler.

'She's gotta be put to the bed!' Petunia insists.

'Most of my babies do, Petunia.' Le Loup winks at her and Petunia shakes her head and smiles self-consciously.

'Bring the holy one in, by all means.' He waves and they carry me in. As we pass Le Loup, he smiles and scans me over like a tray of deli slices.

Pooh is chortling in the background until there's a sudden loud smack and a gasping for air. I look up and see Pooh, bent over, holding her face and Le Loup looking on with the same muted smile.

'I see you got your baptizing sheets all made,' Stella says, pointing to the satin black-and-white zebra sheets they gently lay me onto. 'She won't be needing . . .'

'I understand that,' Le Loup says with a smile but with an undertone of force.

The 3D poster of Pope John Paul II on the ceiling is winking at me in a slightly lascivious way. Everyone is standing around the bed staring at me. I smile and wave like I did to Pooh earlier in the morning.

Two loud hand claps make everyone jump. 'Okay, folks, thanks for bringing her 'round.' Le Loup claps his hands again and everyone starts to file out, humming *We Saw Thee Not* in the key of F.

'So, you're a saint,' Le Loup says in a buried voice, sitting on the bed and leaning over me, his small eyes gleaming with impatience.

I hear Pooh suck her teeth. I don't move.

'Well, Pooh, I guess you're on your own tonight. Hope that Jackalope did you well.'

'Le Loup, you don't believe she's a saint, do you?' Pooh says while moving out of Le Loup's striking range.

Le Loup plays with my curls like a cat toying with a mouse tail.

'It doesn't really matter, does it?' He smiles sideways at her. 'Whore or saint, don't matter. They both bring in money,' he laughs.

Pooh squeezes her fierce eyes at me. I tilt my head into Le Loup's hand.

I practice smiling at Pooh, just like Sarah does when some girl would come charging at her, broken beer bottle thrust out like a torch. I'd wrap my arms around myself and watch Sarah lean deeper into her man's arms, a masklike detached grin float-

ing across her carmine mouth. I'd watch from the corner of the
bar, hidden behind the dusty striated rays of light, as the man
would toss a can at the crying woman and yell at her to go get lost
and Sarah would lick her lips in triumph.

'Get out of here, Pooh,' Le Loup says calmly.

Pooh starts to say something, but Le Loup pulls back his fist,
so she runs out, slamming the door.

'We gotta practice our miracles,' he says, gently tugging at my
hair.

The rain never came that night. The sky boomed, flashed, and
squeezed out a few fat droplets, but no more than that. That miracle was clearly the jurisdiction of a saint triumphing over the
sorcery of a black snake. Some whispered about the ash trees that
burnt up in flashes of lightning, just the sort of conniving sign of
a black snake. But Stella said there is always plenty of heretical
jealous folks around to spread nasty rumors.

Pooh made hardly any money that night as well. All the truckers came to see me, laid out on zebra-striped satin sheets. They
whispered their prayers for a Kenworth's Limited Edition truck
with a heated waterbed in the cab and for the strange burning
sensation in their groin areas to be cast from them. Le Loup lit
candles and shook the trucker's hands a little too hard until they
were more generous in the collection plate.

The TV crews and reporters didn't show up, but all the lizards
still took Mary Kay Cosmetics lessons and stocked up on camera-
friendly earth tones so they would be well prepared.

Pooh told everyone that would listen that she now had the ability to know what every trick wanted without them ever having to
utter an often humiliating word of it. She just knew. The Jackalope had given her the second sight. But not many folks listened.
Le Loup stuffed the money she handed him into his boots then

pushed her away. Pooh would drag her astonished customers up to Le Loup's for them to testify about her extraordinary capabilities, but when her johns saw the glowing halo above my head they were struck dumb. The carefully concealed lights Le Loup had rigged did cast quite a glow, similar to that of the Jackalope's natural effulgence. Le Loup explained that it was necessary to highlight my subtle luminescence for the truckers whose sight had been ruined by driving long night hauls. Pooh's customers would overhear the other truckers attesting to the miracles their visits with me had wrought, and they'd drop to their knees. The large tips they were to hand to Le Loup in gratitude for Pooh's newfound aptitudes were quickly placed on the collection plate — with an extra fifty dollars or so along with an attached prayer that they too might have the blessing of being able to haul overloaded rigs right through weigh stations with nary a blink from an inspector. Pooh would nudge and then slap at her dates to try to bring them around to their original mission. But they ignored her and muttered their praises to me, the new patron saint of truckers. Pooh would try to regale Le Loup with what her johns were to say, then she'd grab at her tip as her trick placed it on the offering plate. I'd shout to her as soon as I saw Le Loup's fist rise back behind him. She'd raise her eyes from the money to look at me, her eyes burning with indignant rage. The fist would get to her before I could find words.

Le Loup never baptized me. He never climbed atop me and took me like a wild animal in the night, as I heard all his lizards tell of as they displayed his claw marks. He never sank his teeth into my neck, giving me his brand for life, depositing his saliva into my blood so the need to sate his appetites would pump through my heart forever with ever-increasing urgency.

Le Loup only pats my head and fluffs my socks. Just like Glad had done. No truckers diddle me, even. Like a museum piece, no one is permitted any physical contact with me, except for private, specially arranged sessions for those who wish to contribute more profusely to the collection plate. As the patron presses my hand to his heart, I close my eyes under the radiating heat from the spotlights. Sometimes the patron squeezes my hand so hard it feels as if it is breaking, but I bite my lip and say nothing that would cause Le Loup to take the touch away.

The dresses Glad had me wearing look like potato sacks next to the frilly, lacy dresses Le Loup has me in. I feel like a doily quilt displayed on the bed.

Le Loup doesn't even touch me to help me get dressed. If I tell him I can't reach a zipper down my back, it goes unzipped.

'He's not wanting to soil you,' Stella says while feeding me in bed, as she does all my meals. 'Once he sees that smooth puerile sacred skin of yours'—she quivers—'well, he might be tempted to baptize you and damn his soul forever.'

'And his fuckin' collection plate,' Pooh spits.

'What's that lump under your blouse?' Le Loup says one day when I'm wearing an unusually tight silken top.

'It's a cross, isn't it? She always wears it,' Petunia tells him. 'It's gotta be one of them folk-made carved crosses, so sweet . . . I always see it through her clothes.'

I nod and try to cover the penis bone outline with my hand.

'It's too big,' Le Loup says while counting out stacks of money. 'I'll buy you a proper dainty one from the Pay Mart.'

I reluctantly take off and toss my raccoon bone out the window and under one of the huge bright-yellow skunk cabbage leaves.

I envy Pooh, in her tight leather miniskirts, sequined silver halters, and precarious heels, handing fatter and fatter wads of money to Le Loup that he, without acknowledging her, stuffs into his boots.

'I hope your innards don't give up on us anytime soon,' Le Loup says through his half grin, after having to install velvet ropes for keeping all my worshippers queued to avoid the fist-fights and sporadic gunshots taken to line jumpers.

'Even desperate lizards on line to see the Jackalope don't need no goddarned gates to keep them in order,' Stella laughs.

'I guess the truckers are more desperate to get the inspectors off their backs than you lizards are to get on yours for a trucker,' Lymon says as he turns over his whole paycheck so he can fondle my feet.

Sometimes, when my palm is resting above one of Pooh's johns' hearts, I can feel my second sight beginning to unfurl. It comes to me in a hazy sensation, like trying to recall a particular scent from childhood. I sense what position they favor, whether they like to be spanked and chastised for being naughty, or what nasty words they are partial to having moaned into their ear.

Pooh stopped bringing in her tricks to testify to Le Loup after a particular trucker she had brought in who hauled an eighteen-wheeler filled with Kingsford charcoal briquettes ended up contributing to have a visit with me. As I pressed my palm to his beaded forehead, I suddenly saw flashes of lustings from the trucker that were so black and deviant I could only shudder and shake. Everyone took my tremors as a sign of divine sanction, and Le Loup later whispered in my ear how I must incorporate that more often. Since I'd never done anything except lie there and occasionally fall asleep, my outburst caused deeper levels of allegiance and adoration toward me. But Pooh knew what had caused my trembling. She saw me staring at the thick fin-ger marks around her neck and the blue pallor her face still carried. Pooh had anticipated what he would do to her. She had used her second sight to know that it was the lack of surprise in her eyes, the lack of struggle on her part that would cause him to lose interest and to loosen his grip. She was the first not to end up face-down in a ditch at the side of the road. His inability to strangle her left him in a sobbing heap and Pooh was able to convince him to tell Le Loup, without mentioning any dead bodies of course. She was truly a psychic lot lizard, and deserving of media attention if anyone was.

I knew Pooh had believed the Kingsford trucker was too dark to be swayed by any God-fearing fervency, but the trucker was so unsteadied by Pooh's lack of terror and his own resulting impotence that, as they approached Le Loup's and he heard other truckers discussing how they were all going to visit the patron saint of truckers, he thought now might be a chance to petition for a return to his old murderously crafty self.

After I had removed my hand from the trucker's head, Pooh and I just stared at each other in silence. Something passed between us, like walking in on someone masturbating in a toilet stall. I had become a part of something private. My body had experienced the fear she had deadened herself to. Likewise, I could feel she now knew something about me. Something secret. Pooh nodded her head solemnly at me as if conceding defeat, but gave an insinuating smile and wink of her eye, indicating that next time she would be the one leaving me in humiliation.

'You're gonna walk on water today,' Le Loup calls down matter-of-factly from high up on a ladder as he changes one of my spotlights before we open for morning worship.

'I never did that before,' I say.

'Well, I'm sure Jesus had a touch of the nerves his first time too.' He laughs his gruff humorless laugh and tosses a burnt-out red bulb next to me.

'A contingent of Baptist truck drivers from up North are coming down to see you. Yankee Baptists!' He spits and it lands near the bulb. 'But they got cash,' he says under his breath as he climbs down the ladder, 'so we're gonna give them a miracle . . .'

I can't help but stare at his oversized hands as they grip the ladder tightly, the same way I've seen him grip one of his girl's wrists as he'd drag her into another room.

'Go get yourself dressed. In that little pink thing I got you. We gotta get the show on the road.' He slaps his hands together and I jump. I've heard those slaps followed by cries from the girls he pulls into the other room. I've heard them beg and apologize and swear whatever will never happen again.

'Let's go!' He claps his hands once more and I jump again. I slide myself off the bed and head to the dressing room that he built for me.

I've waited for him to use his hands on me. I've held out my wrist for him to grab and drag me into the other room. I even spilled cherry cola on my white pinafore on purpose. I knew he whipped Pooh for putting runs too fast into the stockings he had bought her. I sat on the edge of the bed and watched his face turn the shade of turnip tops, and his hands open and close like a caught fish gasping for air. I just sat there and waited. Just like I would do with Sarah. After she'd come home after being gone for a week or more and she'd just float in and say nothing to me, I'd go into her suitcase and take out something that meant something to her, and I'd hurt it. Lay it out for her to see, slashed and bleeding with her ketchup from one of her little packs. I'd sit and wait for her to notice. I'd also lay the belt out next to me.

Le Loup just grunted and snorted like he was a vacuum with some blockage.

'This cost a lot didn't it?' I said, sounding as careless as I could and holding myself back from apologizing.

'Umm!' he grunted.

'Are you mad at me?' I said, making my tone as cloying as possible.

Le Loup stood stiffly with his back to me. His fists tightened and I felt breathless as he slowly turned to me on his heels.

'Tell Pooh to get her ass in to see me as soon as she gets here.' He smiled tightly at me, the hollows alongside his mouth looking like deep, empty canyons.

Later that day I heard him slapping Pooh because she had shut the door too loudly.

I never provoked him on purpose after that.

The sun has just nearly descended when Le Loup finishes his Baptist-tailored sermon and I emerge from my hiding place behind a thick patch of hemlock, spruce, and myrtle trees. Le Loup has set up his trick lighting hid under the alder, laurel, and willow shrubs, so there is an eerie red-lit haze obscuring the murky water in front of me. Twenty or so Yankee truckers are standing on the bank opposite me, clutching Bibles with one hand and their falsified logbooks with the other.

Stella and Petunia are at my side. They have as much contempt for Yankee truckers, Baptist wannabe's, as any of the Three Crutches folk, plus they are well acquainted with indulging themselves in the petty sin of a paltry ruse in the interest of commerce.

'Not much different than telling a john he makes me come so hard my eyes almost knock loose!' Petunia pointed out.

Le Loup added, 'Supernatural occurrences never happen up North, because Yanks have no space left in their hearts, in their minds, and on their land for a miracle of the Lord to have a chance to take seed.'

Everyone nodded furiously in agreement.

'That's why they all flock down here to borrow our divine manifestations!' Lymon snapped.

'Well, there's enough miraculous occurrences here to share, even with Yanks,' Le Loup said while patting his wallet.

And as those Yanks sat in the diner, no one pointed out to them the new menus printed up with triple the prices. And nobody offered the teary-eyed Yanks a lemon wedge or a blessed spray of the healing mist for their burning eyes, except for a small courtesy fee, which was neither small nor extended with much courtesy.

As I gaze at the Yankee truckers lined up on the other side of the bog, I notice all of them swabbing frantically at their wet eyes. But whether that's from the moving fervent adoration of Le Loup's oration or the open potato sack full of fresh-cut ramps, which lies hidden in the cotton grass behind them, is anybody's guess.

Gasps rise from the audience as I move more into view.

Le Loup had finally settled on putting me in a charming little German dirndl with matching red velvet bows in my hair. Mary Grace did my makeup using her new Mary Kay products. I felt the pride a trucker must feel in taking a virgin, watching Mary Grace's finger leave its prints on the unblemished pressed powder's surfaces, the plastic protective shields cast to the ground.

Le Loup invites the truckers to toss heavy rocks attached to fishing lines into the water to prove there is no hidden platform beneath the surface of the water.

The rocks splash, cast in at various depths of the water. We all watch in silence as the reels spin out after the rocks until the spindles are emptied.

'Gentlemen, as you can see . . .' Le Loup announces.

'There is no platform under there,' one of the northerners certifies and they all murmur agreement.

'Maybe that little girl should be wearing a lifejacket,' another one of them says.

'That would take out all the fun . . .' someone grumbles back to him.

Lymon hits the play button on the cassette deck and blasts *Hallelujah, Praise Jehovah!* which is my cue to raise my arms straight up and allow Stella and Petunia to lift me into the air.

I wiggle my bare toes and feet as if in a devout fervor, which also serves the dual purpose of authenticating there are no rafts or other flotation devices set upon my feet.

The music lowers and Le Loup starts reading the scripture.

I am going to walk, I tell myself, and place my toes into the murky, cold water.

'Whatever you do, just keep moving,' Petunia and Stella whisper in my ears.

'You keep moving,' Le Loup had also advised. 'You sink, no one is coming in after you . . .'

I stare out at the men across the bog. They've got their arms spread out to me, like fathers encouraging their baby to take his first steps into their arms.

My body jerks involuntarily at the sense memory, of once having taken those steps into somebody's arms . . .

I let go of the hands holding me and take a big step farther out into the cool musky water, and I slowly start to sink.

'Walk to me, walk to me,' I hear echoing under the praises to Jesus.

I quickly take another wobbly step as the water climbs to my ankles. I lift my feet high and step again . . . and I hear the round of gasps as I start to sink and panic begins to take hold of me.

'Keep moving!' I hear from behind me.

The gnarl of mosquitoes buzzing in my ear and the excitement in the truckers' voices grow as the water rises to my knees.

One of the truckers twenty-five feet in front of me squats down and spreads his arms out to me wider.

I raise up my bare right foot and take another step.

He nods at me and smiles warmly, as if he were willing me the raw determination to reach him.

I follow with my left foot and to my surprise, I am buoyant. I feel a soft cloud beneath me. I take another step and I am walking. I am walking on the water. And I am heading toward him, the man wiggling his fingers at me.

The music blasts louder as I coast across the surface of the water. Some of the truckers wave their Bibles, some their logbooks. They all cheer.

His eyes are hazel like the pliant bark of a slippery elm. I am five feet in front of the welcoming arms of the squatting man, and it is only Le Loup's loud clearing of his throat that keeps me from bolting the rest of the way into the man's arms.

I take my steps, moving forward steadily, gracefully as we had practiced before at Le Loup's.

Two more steps and I will be in his arms and nothing will matter any more. I will forgive his long absence, I won't even ask why he left, or if he ever thought of me or missed me the way I missed him.

The jubilance of the crowd is masked by my heart surging in all its electrical currents toward him. I take one more step onto the dry land and he is there in front of me. Le Loup shouts a loud 'Hallelujah!' I open my arms to the man as he suddenly pops up and turns from me to slap hands with some of the other truckers. 'You lost that one, buddy!' he says. 'You owe me two hundred dollars now!' He high-fives some hands and whoops 'Hallelujah!' and 'Fuckin' A!'

Logbooks get pressed into my hands. 'I rode straight for a solid week without a break. Please bless this falsified logbook!' petitions one trucker on his knees.

'Me too!' another pleads.

'Gentlemen!' shouts Le Loup, instantly hushing the crowd. 'You may have an audience with Saint Sarah back at the church.' The church was Le Loup's barn, now stripped of the fur and the wet-animal scent. The wood floor had been spread with sawdust, and urns of imported incense burned on little plywood mantels. The satin zebra sheets had been replaced with bedding more fitting for a saint. Even the 3D picture of the Pope was removed, with apologies muttered by Le Loup. 'Too confusing to the various Christ-loving factions,' Le Loup explained.

Lymon wraps a big towel around me and starts to turn me away from the crowd. I look for the man over my shoulder and see him taking money from another man's hand.

'You did it, honey,' Lymon mumbles into my ear and kneels down to tenderly dry my feet. His fingers lovingly glide over my toes, picking off the bits of the sphagnum moss that made my walk on water possible. For the first time I am not overwhelmed to the point of nausea by his strong onion-garlic ramp smell.

I touch him back. I let my fingers run through the hard loofah-like surface of his crew cut. He lets out a subdued moan, stops moving, and presses his arms against my calves. I move my fingers to his shoulders and along the stringlike tendons that seem stretched to their limits as he drops his neck to my thighs. His hands tremble and he peers up at me with flat timid eyes filled with tears.

'It's been so long . . .' he whispers.

'I know. And I'm sorry I left you,' I say and caress his cheek.

'You two lovebirds better get a move on,' Pooh whispers behind us, 'before he sees . . .' She gestures at Le Loup behind her.

'Pooh, I didn't know you were here,' I say, surprised.

'We don't usually get this much holy fire until the Ramps Festival.' Pooh winks at me, and Lymon scurries away silently. 'Couldn't miss it. Let's get you back.' Pooh puts her arm around me and leads me through the marshy ground to Le Loup's Trans Am.

'Pooh, I'm really sorry this all got so . . .' I suddenly feel a strong desire to reach for her hand, but it's playing with some necklace under her shirt.

'Oh, now don't you worry yourself,' she says. 'Things have a way of working out.' She smiles and I think I catch a hint of slick animosity under her wide grin. Pooh takes her hand out from beneath her shirt and pats my hand.

'Oh, been meaning to show you . . .' She reaches inside the neck of her shirt. 'I got something I've been wanting you to take a look-see at.' She slowly pulls up on a leather thong. 'Check this out.' At first I think it's a furless rabbit's foot, then my eyes focus on it and I see it's a raccoon penis bone.

'Isn't it great?!' Pooh says, dangling it in front of me.

My first thought is she earned one too. Glad must've somehow heard of her fame and rewarded her. 'You got one too?' I say.

'Pardon?' she says and cocks her head.

'Uh, where'd you get that?' I try to say mildly.

'I found it.' Her smile grows bigger.

Unconsciously my hand searches my neck for my raccoon penis bone, and then I picture myself tossing it out the window into . . .

'Funniest thing too,' Pooh laughs a little too loud.

I nod and, as if I'm in on what's so funny, I give a hollow smile.

'Le Loup lets the skunk cabbage grow around the house all

winter 'cause it naturally gives out more heat than a goat's butt in a pepper patch . . . melts the snow real nice so I don't gotta get out to shovel . . .'

I feel a saw blade of fear creep up my spine.

'But come the warm weather, he has me get out the machete and chop it out afore the stink gets worse than a hog farm in August.'

As Pooh rambles on, my head keeps nodding like a spring-loaded souvenir doll.

'So, when I was hacking away'—Pooh slices the air with her hand—'I found this necklace in the skunk bushes. It was in the ones under the window out back, ya know, near your bed?'

'Did you show it to him?' I ask, trying to keep my voice nonchalant.

'Oh, your feet are all bleeding . . .' she says, pointing at them.

I glance at them and nod. 'I didn't notice.'

'It's all the pitcher plants, sundews, and bladder worts. They eat flesh. That's how a lot of bodies get disposed of around here.' Pooh shrugs. 'In those bogs'—she gestures to where I had just performed my miracle—'you float on the moss, like swinging in a hammock, while them plants chew you up nice and slow . . .'

'Did you show it to him?' I repeat between shallow breaths.

'No. Should I? What's it mean?' Pooh narrows her perpetually swollen eyes at me.

I stare at the little bloody bites on my feet. 'It just means I once worked for someone else.'

'I've been asking around about it.'

'What'd ya hear?'

'Just . . . nothing. I don't ask everyone. I just didn't have a clue who it could've belonged to . . .' Pooh blinks her eyes in rapid succession. 'Who'd you work for?'

'Just someone I don't work for now,' I say and turn to the glass
to see Le Loup heading toward the car.

'Uh-huh . . . Look'—Pooh takes my hand—'I don't hate you,
okay? I'm not trying to mess you. We can work together, 'kay?'

I regard her and nod as Le Loup pulls open the door.

'Some fucking show!' he says climbing into the driver's seat,
while Pooh inconspicuously slips the raccoon penis bone under
her shirt. 'Those Yanks is forkin' over like they just been shown
the afterworld!' He reaches over Pooh and caresses my head.
Pooh coughs.

'The plants tried to eat her up,' Pooh says and points to my
bleeding feet.

'Ahh, we got a new stigmata! Sure beats the fuck out of onion
tears, don't it!' Le Loup laughs and we drive off.

One day Pooh starts playing Barbies with me. Le Loup was out
on his recruiting trips, looking for new lizards he could lure away
from their respective lot daddies. Pooh kneels down on the floor
near my bed where I'm resting after a long morning of blessing
truckers. Without a word she slides out the vinyl cases of dolls.
She lifts them onto the bed and sits next to them.

'Damn, you've been busier than a cat covering crap on a marble floor, collecting all these dolls,' Pooh laughs.

'They're okay.' I shrug.

'When I was little all I wanted was Barbies.' Pooh sighs and
her eyes take on a rare distant softness. 'When Le Loup bought
me from my uncle, he promised he'd get me so many Barbies I
wouldn't have room to fart,' she says slowly, taking out the dolls
and laying them tenderly on the bed.

'How much he buy you for?'

'Fuck knows. Probably a case of beer. I woulda gone with him for free.' She looks puzzled as she examines one of the garishly dressed Barbies.

'How'd you meet him?' I take out Dentist Barbie and subtly wave her around to try to interest Pooh.

Pooh crinkles her nose as she turns the Barbie around in her hand. 'Uncle sold Le Loup his corn liquor, but it was really just Sterno that we would pour through loaves of Wonder bread to clean it up some.' Pooh creases her brow and begins to lift the little Lycra skirt of the Barbie.

'Did Le Loup find out?' I quickly reach under the bed for the Barbie mobile and start driving it up to Pooh to get her to seat the doll in it.

'My uncle'd be sucking chrome off a trailer hitch if he ain't had me to offer to Le Loup.' She ignores the car and starts to work down the fuchsia tights on the Barbie. 'But, Lord, was Le Loup sweet to me. I was his baby.' She sighs and her hands fall still for a moment. 'But faster than a feather singeing in hell, I started to let him down.' She looks up at me and her eyes darken as if she's remembering a secretly held thought. 'Like how he treats you.' She looks at me so directly I can only lower my eyes.

'Here, look at this one. She's got a belly button ring,' I say and try to hand Pooh another Barbie from the case.

While holding my gaze. Pooh pulls down the doll's tights with a firm tug. She grabs other similarly dressed ones, pulls up their dresses, and pulls down their tights. An eerie smile spreads across Pooh's face. I look down at a line of Ken dolls lying between us. Their skirts or dresses are hitched over their heads, exposing their little naked U plastic penises or their painted-on underwear, looking like a row of fainted cross-dressed flashers.

'I thought it was funny,' I say quietly and offer her a half smile.

'It is,' she says, keeping the same disquieting grin on her face.

'I know you mean more to Le Loup than I ever could,' I say.

'What're you talking about?' She shakes her head and smiles at me with her mouth sealed.

'He—he never touches me, never . . .'

'What's this?' she says, looking at me again and holding up one of the doll's Q-Tip raccoon penis bones I had made.

I blow out a big sigh of air, 'Umm, they're, just necklaces.'

Pooh's mouth goes askew slightly then resumes its former shape. She claps her hands just like Le Loup does and I drop the doll I'm holding between my legs.

Her hand forms a vise and she reaches for the fallen doll. I snatch it up and hold it in front of my private parts. She delicately reaches over and lifts the dolls away from me, and as she does she snaps the splayed rubbery legs of the Barbie under my skirt and against the cotton crotch of my panties. 'Whoops . . . sorry . . .'

Pooh and I play with our dolls whenever Le Loup is away.

Pooh shows up one day holding a thread-worn folded-over patch of red velvet.

'I have something special.' She points with a tilt of her head to the dolls I have already laid out for us. I raise my eyebrows in anticipation. She sits on the bed next to me and slowly opens the velvet square as if she were uncovering a smuggled treasure. I see bits of chicken bones mixed with gold thread.

'Those Q-tips really don't look right,' she says reaching in with her pinky finger and scooping out one of her creations. She holds out on the nail of her pinky finger a miniature necklace.

'I made more realistic raccoon penis bones,' she says and winks at me. It's the first time I ever heard her admit she knew exactly what the necklaces were. 'Lymon gave me some boiled chicken bones. I hacked chips off of them and I got some gold thread from Stella.' She reaches for the doll I'm holding, a Ken doll dressed in Flight Attendant Barbie's gray linen uniform dress. Pooh puts the new necklace on the doll and hands her back to me.

I give Pooh a weak grin. 'What did they say?'

'They? Who? Lymon and Stella? Never asked what it was for . . . why?' Pooh jingles the diminutive necklaces.

I nod, then shrug. 'I just think we should keep this, ya know, private.' I start pulling the old dental-floss Q-Tip necklaces off the dolls.

'It's nobody's business,' she says in a low voice that resembles a growl. 'Now, I have to run over your flight attendant there for stealing Rock Star Ken,' she says matter-of-factly.

'That was like a month ago. Rock Star Ken has been back with your Ballerina Barbie since then,' I protest.

'Still gotta be a payback. Just because I bided my time doesn't mean she's getting away with it.' Pooh snatches the doll from my hand, grabs the Barbie car, lays my doll flat, and proceeds to run her over, back and forth. 'Steal my man, you bitch cunt whore,' Pooh chants under her breath. I watch in silence as she rips off my doll's clothes and then decapitates and delimbs her. 'Try that again, cunt,' she whoops.

Pooh calmly wipes away a lock of hair that fell into her face, brushes her hands together, and smiles a relieved smile. 'So what do you want to play today?' she says in her sweetest voice.

Pooh and I don't play much after that. I usually say I'm sick or tired. And finally I ask Le Loup to take the dolls in their vinyl cases away, saying I've overheard some of the truckers wondering why a messenger from the Lord would play with Barbies.

'I knew it!' he yells, raising his voice to me for the first time.

Business has been slowing down. Fewer and fewer truckers show up every day. Some truckers have even summoned up the guts to ask Le Loup for their money back, citing an increase in being pulled over by Highway Patrol, their logbooks inspected with a fine-tooth comb, and having scales overweigh their haul, even when their rig was half empty, all after they had had a visitation with me. After a few truckers leave with shoe prints and large indents in the seats of their pants, no refunds are requested again.

Le Loup puts in flashier lights, but the crowds thin as talk spreads of luck turning malevolent after a visit with me, the patron saint of truckers.

I don't even have to tell Pooh that Le Loup has taken the dolls. She just suddenly stops flopping down on my bed to try to cajole me into playing. At first I feel relief, but soon I began to miss her company.

As the wads of cash that Pooh turns over have grown fatter, Le Loup can no longer ignore her growing fame as a lot lizard with blessed second sight. The truckers who used to wait to see me now line their trucks in a queue that stretches out of the truck stop and runs along the highway for some distance.

For the first time I really start to put some effort into my sainthood. I incorporate every enigmatic phenomenon I have ever observed. I shake my body attempting to mimic the supernatural way Mother Shaprio's massive body pulsated when she laughed. I roll my eyes the way I'd seen truckers do in the mysterious throes of climax, and I claw at the air the way I'd seen Sarah do in her epileptic-like fits of rage. I even place my palm on the heads of kneeling truckers and mutter the bits of mangled Choctaw chants that Glad would bless his lizards with before each night of work. And while my newfound gusto picks up business a little, it never brings the *World News* or any camera crews over. And it isn't long before even my most steady worshipers take their business to Pooh.

'After I seen Saint Sarah for the tenth time, I got five blown-out wheels in a row and I still can't love my wife proper!' I over hear one trucker warning another. 'Now, after I'd seen that Saint Pooh, well, my tires stopped blowin' out and when I see my wife I'm always hard as honeymoon dick.'

'That's for me. I'm heading to Saint Pooh.' I hear them walk away.

'Saint Pooh.' I shake my head and let out a little sarcastic laugh.

'Least she don't need no trick lighting,' Le Loup says in a low grumble, surprising me from behind.

He leans above me, reaches his hand down, his fingernails extended, and lets his arm swing over me like a pendulum with an ax attached to its tip.

'You've started to cost me . . .'

'I can work like Pooh,' I whisper up to him, following his hand barely grazing my stomach. 'I saw the Jackalope too. I can develop my second sight too.'

In a flash I see his fist blazing toward me. My stomach clenches and I close my eyes and steel my face for the impact.

The wall shatters next to my bed and I open my eyes to see Le Loup pulling his hand out of the splintered hole his fist has made. He cradles his hand like a paw wounded in a blade trap and stalks out silently.

I get up slowly and my body aches as if I had just taken his beating. Nobody is waiting to have a visit with me and a tray of food is sitting on the table for me. Stella no longer cradles me in her arms to feed me like her lapbaby, since she finally accepted the camera crews were not to come and all her TV-friendly shades of clothes and makeup was money wasted. The only words she says to me are to recount all the miracles Pooh is reported to have achieved. Blind men coming so hard it unblocks their retinas, the lame having their spinal cord so electrified they can now do gymnastics, and the true miracle of Pooh suck-starting a Harley, which might bring the camera crews yet. I look at the food—a huge mound of ramps and liver fry.

'Might as well feed her ramps,' Petunia had told Le Loup. 'Ain't no one to be offended by her gas anyhows.'

I walk to the window in the back, the one I had flung my raccoon penis bone out of, and push it open. I squint at the brightness I'm unaccustomed to. To help give me a saintly ghostly pallor, Le Loup forbid me to venture out until the sun sets, though I'm hardly ever allowed out even then.

'I've seen truckers who only night-drive with third-degree burns from the moon's reflection,' Le Loup told me. But even when the moon was away or hidden by thick fog, I was to stay in. 'Plenty of pimps wouldn't mind stealing my saint away,' he said, locking the door behind him.

A sweet breeze of bog rosemary, moss, and coniferous trees, with an underlying trail of diesel slides across my face. I picture Glad's arms spread out to receive me, his hands holding a slightly bigger bone to reward my impressive, though unsuccessful, initiative. I imagine a big welcome-back party for me at The Doves, all my old customers weeping with joyful anticipation of being able to show me their new underwear in the girlish pastel colors of Lucky Charms cereal. Even Mother Shapiro would defrost some of the delectable treasures from her freezer to celebrate my return. But what makes me suddenly push half my body out the window is the thought of Sarah's face. Her eyes, ringed red with tears from missing me, help me to propel my right leg out of the window frame.

I look down at the chopped-up skunk cabbage under the window and am pretty sure it will cushion my drop from eight feet up. I need to wipe Sarah's tears and promise never to leave her again.

I push up and begin to bring my left leg to the sill, but it catches on something. I pull at my foot, but it stays stuck. I whip my face around inside the room to see what I'm stuck on.

'Where're you heading?' Le Loup says without asking. He's holding on to my foot with his hand.

'I—I . . .' My eyes blink like a stuttered word. 'I just wanted some air.' I squeeze out.

'Get on your bed and lay there. You have a customer.' Le Loup holds his arm up, pointing toward my show-bed in the next room. I extricate myself and follow his direction silently.

Later that day as I lie staring at the darker shade of unfaded paint where the Pope poster had been, I hear hammering and the clang of metal.

'I put gates on all the windows, so if you need to get any air you might want to try the front door first,' Le Loup says and leaves, slamming the door behind him. I watch the locks turn as he seals me in with his keys.

I run to the windows as soon as I hear his car pull away. Thick bars hang from every window. I wrap my hands around them and scream.

I scream and scream until folks gather beneath the window to see what in all hell's the matter. I keep screaming even when they run and fetch Stella who has a copy of the keys. I keep screaming even as she comes behind me and puts her hand over my mouth. I bite at her hand and thrash my feet, hitting onlookers in the face, groin, and shins. I scream and kick out even harder as I see Petunia heading toward me with a big fat syringe that I heard she usually uses on herself.

'Quick, hold her arm!' Stella directs one of the men trying to keep my limbs still.

I feel a sharp jab in my shoulder and warmth spread through my arm.

'I told you she was really a black snake.' I hear the dishwasher hiss as I struggle to keep fighting.

'You can never underestimate the power of a black snake to charm and change forms,' Mary Grace says, peeping her head up from behind the dishwasher.

The room starts to slant and fade. My muscles slacken and I fall into the hands pinning me down. Before my eyes close I see Lymon looking at me with his head tilted and his eyes filled with empathic warmth, like a passerby mourning a car-hit deer being moved to the side of the road.

'Wake up, c'mon, wake up!' I feel something shaking at my side and I open my eyes to watch a gigantic shiny black snake swallow my entire arm. I bolt up screaming, shaking the snake off me.

'Grab her, grab her, grab her!' I turn to see Lymon reaching out and Pooh pointing at me. I look at my arms and can't find the snake.

'Where's the snake?' I gasp and let myself collapse into Lymon's arms.

'Well, you're the snake is what I heard tell,' Pooh says with a small smile playing on her lips.

'Aw, she ain't no snake, she ain't no saint, she just a baby girl that needs some lovin' is all,' Lymon says and pats my hand in his quivering hand.

'Well, they all think you're a snake,' Pooh says nonchalantly. 'Except Lymon here, and me of course,' she adds.

I stare up at Pooh and notice for the first time her face isn't swollen and her hair has all grown in, no bald patches. 'You look great, Pooh,' I whisper.

'She quit drinking,' Lymon says.

'I'm almost the most famous lizard in all of North America!' Pooh says, annoyed. 'Drinking has nothin' to do with anything. But, yeah, I don't drink no more.' She puts her hands triumphantly on her hips.

'I heard, Pooh. Congratulations.' I reach out my limp hand for her to shake.

'Thank you.' Pooh squeezes my hand hard.

'Le Loup must be so proud of you,' I say.

Pooh gives me a look, but with her face partially averted and her lids half-drawn, I can't catch it.

'You're the one living here in his house,' she says slowly, as if I don't speak English.

'I think he's gonna throw me out any minute, Pooh.' I push myself up out of Lymon's arms. 'I wish he would, so I can join you.' I try to smile at her. Since Pooh had stopped coming to play, I often daydreamed about us living in our own trailer, playing dolls and having a red neon sign out front so folks would all know where to find the most famous lizards. 'I can't wait to develop my second sight too.'

'First off, what makes you think you can be as good as me?' Pooh says, leaning over me. Her breath gives off a sweet grass scent, and not the usual rubbing alcohol smell.

'I saw the Jackalope too,' I say.

'What's with you?' Pooh tilts her head at me. 'You want to steal everything I own, don't ya?!'

'Girls,' Lymon says and gently pulls me back, down onto his lap. 'Now, Pooh came to me to help save you.'

Pooh smoothes out her new slick black leather dress and pats her hair in a ladylike manner.

'Lymon is the only one that has a key copy besides Stella,' Pooh says.

'Won't Le Loup be here any time now?' I ask.

'Nope.' Lymon shakes his head in his sad donkey way. 'After the truckers have a visit with Pooh here, they are so shocked by the strength of their awakened passions, only large quantities of drink will calm them.'

Pooh nods proudly.

'Even with all the local stills pumping as much white lightning as possible, Le Loup still had to gather a few men and hunt down more.'

I turn and look at a jailed window. 'Why don't Le Loup just turn me out? I'm not making any money for him here.'

'Well, for one' — Pooh bends back one of her fingers — 'if he turns you out, that would be admitting he knew you weren't no saint. Nobody turns a real saint out to whore these days.' She bends back two fingers. 'Plus, folk really think you're just black magic.'

Lymon flaps his head again. 'Your miracles have all turned sour, they say. I try to tell 'em you're just a little girl needin' lovin'.'

'Ain't no trucker gonna put his piss pump anywheres into a black snake!' Pooh snorts.

'Anyways, it's bad for Le Loup's stature in the pimp community.'

'Plus, some folks say he's sweet on you,' Lymon says slyly.

'I severely doubt that, Lymon!' Pooh snaps.

Lymon shakes his head earnestly. 'Has he ever hit you?' He leans around to face me, his breath coming at me in minted-over ramp freshness.

I shake my head no.

'He ever touch ya?' Lymon wags his head.

I shake my head again.

'He watch ya get dressed?'

I again shake my head.

'But he buys you all kinds of lacy little pretty things, don't he?' Lymon chuckles to himself.

'Don't prove nothin'!' Pooh winces.

'He lay your clothes out for ya?' Lymon's voice goes breathless and high. 'Even your darling little panties? I know he don't give 'em to us to wash like the rest of his laundry . . .'

Pooh sways her head in a long disbelieving sweep and rocks back on the heels of her high-heeled pumps. 'Stop, Lymon.' Pooh's voice sounds splintered and loose like a piece of driftwood not yet worn smooth.

'I says he does those little sweet things himself, by his own hand!' Lymon squeals and convulses with pleasure at the thought.

'Shut up, Lymon! Shut up!' Pooh pulls back her hand to slap his face, but the look of utter horror on Lymon's face stops her. 'Shut up,' she repeats quietly.

'He hangs them on a clothes line behind one of the locked doors,' I say softly to Lymon, avoiding Pooh's eyes.

We sit there in complete silence, just the crickets and the bog mosquitoes starting to fill the dusky light filtering in past the window bars.

'Well, Lymon,' Pooh finally says, her voice slightly hoarse, 'every now and then, even a blind pig finds an acorn. Maybe you're right, okay? Maybe Le Loup does love her, but it ain't gonna last. I know him deep in, better than you, and I know he loves money more than any pretty little girl!' She spits the last word out at me.

'That's the difference 'tween me and him,' Lymon nods.

'So, She-Ra, Sarah, or whoever you are . . .' Pooh closes her eyelids and I can see her eyes rolling around like shot marbles. She pops her eyes open and spreads a warm smile on her face. She reaches out for my hand and holds it like it's a delicate little gecko that might crawl away 'I missed playing dolls with you,' she says, her voice suddenly tender.

I feel hungry for the warmth in the voice. 'I did too,' I tell her and look away.

'I think you should go home.' But the sweetness in her voice overshadows something bitter, like sugar poured over absinthe.

'I want to,' I say. 'I want to go home.'

Pooh nods her approval, and some of the threat leaves her eyes. 'Lymon is gonna help you. He's gonna take you home.'

Lymon grins, showing his patchwork of tobacco-stained teeth. 'I'll take you home.' He pats my hand.

'I'm here with your food,' Stella announces, entering the barn and setting the plate on the table with a bang. She raises her head to find me on my pedestal bed across the room. 'Lymon, Pooh, what the hell you doin' in here?'

'We was just passing by and heard some hissing in here, had to see if she'd changed form yet!' Lymon says.

'Had she?' Stella asks, wide-eyed, and points to the bare feet sticking out from under my blankets.

'No, she still had her human form on.'

'Ugh!' Stella shudders. 'Pooh, you got them lined up a dozen deep. Maybe you should get on back to work afore a riot breaks.'

'We're just leaving,' Lymon says and pulls up on the black scarf obscuring Pooh's face.

'Did she wake yet?' Stella asks. 'Maybe I ought to check and make sure she is okay. Le Loup might just end up feeding her to the swamp plants but he wouldn't want any of us beating him to it!' Stella laughs.

'I done checked her. She's all fine.' Lymon grins.

'I bet you did, Lymon. I bet you did check her. She okay, Pooh?'

Pooh nods.

'I was afraid Petunia dosed her too high. Well, I am relieved y'all are here. I was afraid she'd be awake and try to charm me like she has before. Wish we'd've tied her down, but Le Loup is the only one likes to do that,' Stella snorts.

Pooh and Lymon nod.

'Well, we better get a move on.' Lymon puts out his arm for Stella.

'See you later, black snake!' Stella calls over her shoulder and lets Lymon usher her to the door. She unlocks it and escorts Lymon and Pooh out.

Now, if Stella had herself stopped drinking, she might've taken note that Pooh was a good half a foot smaller and slighter than she usually was. And if Stella wasn't a major contributor herself to the scarcity of sugar whiskey to be had at Three Crutches, she might've also even caught the hint of golden ringlets peeking out from beneath the scarf, reflecting off the barn door's nightlight like a coin tossed into the air. If the possibility of deprivation of her precious drink hadn't led her to store as much of it away in her cupboards and in her person, well, she might've noticed the silver gypsy rings on the toes sticking out from under the blanket. But all Stella could see were shadows and outlines. She trusted memory for knowing how to move and where to place things.

As Stella unwittingly locks Pooh in Le Loup's barn she tells Lymon and me how she heard folks telling of burning that snake out if Le Loup don't get to it soon enough.

'Too many truckers have had their trucks inspected lately,' she says. 'Someone has to pay. And they're all up at the diner, torches ready to go!'

'Oh, I think that snake is gonna slide back home by its lonesome,' Lymon tells her and pats her back gently so as not to knock her precarious balance out of whack.

Lymon waves goodbye to Stella, then puts his trembling arm around me and we walk off into the truck stop night.

'Are they gonna burn up Pooh?' I ask as he escorts me into his dilapidated tin shack.

'She's not even there any more. I saw her let herself out with my keys when we weren't half out of sight. Believe me, Pooh ain't one to keep her business waiting.' He gropes around in the air, then yanks a chain that clicks on a flickering bulb.

'It's all talk anyhows. Ain't nobody would mess with anything of Le Loup's.'

I nod and let out a long sigh and look around at the bare little room. There's only a military made-up narrow cot, a large mirror shard on top of a steamer trunk, and some taped-up magazine pictures on the walls.

'Besides, rumor has it Le Loup was once a wolf himself, practicing his own kind of black magic.'

'Are you gonna drive me tonight?' I ask and catch a glimpse of myself in the shiny black leather outfit Pooh pulled out of her rucksack for me to borrow. I can't help but run my hands admiringly along the glossy leather.

'I like ya better in that pink dress you got on under there.'

'I don't,' I laugh. 'But I better take Pooh's clothes off and leave them for her. Don't want her coming after me.'

'Yeah, and she would . . . You should take that ugly thing off anyway. You're too sweet to be dressing all naughty and dangerous.' I ignore the high-pitched tone Lymon's voice takes.

I start to slide off Pooh's clothes.

'Here, lemme help ya.' Lymon reaches out his hand so I can

step out of the leather. I hesitantly put my hand in his. 'And take them pumps off.' He squats down and tugs the pumps off as I raise each foot. 'I like those Mary Janes you wear,' he says and digs them out of the rucksack Pooh gave me.

I look over his head at the pictures pinned up on the wall. They're all torn-out magazine ads of little girls in frilly dresses, little girls in swimsuits, and little girls in underwear.

'Lymon . . .' I pat his head and he leans into me. 'We really better go. I wanna go home.'

'Just, please.' He wraps his arms around my legs. 'I ain't loved a pretty little girl in so long.' He sobs and burrows his face into the crinoline of my dress.

'Lymon, they're gonna find out I escaped and come looking for me.' I hold my hands above his head, not wanting to touch him further.

'Stella ain't gonna be by there till the morrow to bring ya eggs by.' He tugs on the hem of my dress like a little kid begging for his mommy to stay. 'I just, it's been so long, since way afore the penitentiary,' he mumbles into the fabric.

'What got ya in the penitentiary, Lymon?'

He leans down to kiss my feet. 'God, how I miss tiny baby-girl feet.' Lymon's voice gets that high sheen to it.

'Lymon.' I put my hands on his head, but he shudders, so I remove them fast like I hit a hot stove. 'Lymon, they're talking burning me up. Now I don't want to burn up or get fed to the plants or anything 'cept go home now!' I reach for my Mary Janes to try to put them on. Lymon grasps my hand and falls on the floor holding it.

'Please, please!' he cries. 'I've loved you since I first seen ya. I tole them all you ain't a snake. I won't let no one hurt ya ever, ever!' He bangs his forehead against the floor. 'I ain't gonna put nothin' inside ya, I just want to hold ya some, look at ya, that's all, that's all!' Lymon knocks his head harder on the floorboards.

'Lymon . . .' I say with a pleading whisper.

'You don't know what it's like. I'm sorry if I disgust ya, I can't help it. I tried in prison, I spoke to all their doctors, and they took everything out of me, years and years, tole them everything.' His forehead is starting to leave little flecks of blood with each bang. 'They let me out, but I knew *it weren't out of me! I can't help it! I love you!*'

'Lymon, stop banging your head. Lymon, you're bleeding.' I squat down and grab his head between my hands.

'I'm sorry!' He wails again and relaxes his head into my hands. 'I just need just a little, then I'll take you right home. No one will know. I'll take ya right home, just ten minutes . . .'

'Lymon,' I sigh, exasperated.

'Five! Five minutes, that's all! And I'll give ya' — he reaches backward into his pocket — 'one hundred, no, two hundred dollars!' He waves a wad of bills at me. 'I been so lonely,' he whines.

I look down at him, peering up at me, like a dog waiting for its owner to signal its next trick.

'I know what it's like to be lonely, Lymon.' I look at the money and think it would be good to come home with something to give to Sarah. I take the money from him and place it in one of my empty Mary Janes.

'Oh, bless you, bless you. You are a saint, a savior.'

'So I've been told.' I sigh again. 'Five minutes . . .'

'Oh, yes!' he says, jumping to his feet. 'Oh, yes! Now, sit here on my bed for a bit.' His voice is quivering and its timbre is starting to elevate again. I sit on his bed and he kneels in front of me.

'I'm just gonna unbutton these sweet little buttons on your sweet little pink dress here . . .' With fingers shaking like a detoxing drunk, he slowly pops my buttons open.

'Five minutes, Lymon,' I remind him.

'Yes, I know, I know. Just let me see . . . oh, oh.' He gasps like a man that just lost a million-dollar bet.

'What?'

'Oh, break my heart!'

'What's wrong?'

'You have on one of them sweet white undie shirts, with a sweet little baby-blue bow at the tippy top!' Tears stream down his face. 'I'm so happy!' He looks up at me, the lines on his face relaxing so he looks ten years younger. 'I could die now.'

'I'm glad I made ya happy, Lymon.' I smile at him.

'Let's'—his voice crackles, it's so high—'let's take that undie, undie shirt off, please, please?'

'Sure, Lymon, I'll take it off for ya.' I pull my arms out of the dress top and start to slide off the undershirt when he stops me.

'Oh, honey, go slow, please. I been dreamin' of this too long to have it go too fast. I wanna get my five minutes' worth. Can you lie yourself down here?' I lie on the thin mattress of his cot. He leans over me. I pull my undershirt down and slowly reraise it.

'Oh, is that ya belly button?' he singsongs like he's talking to an infant. 'Can I—can I kiss it?'

'Sure, go ahead, Lymon.'

He lets out a squeal. He slowly lowers his head, and his hot breath on my stomach tickles and makes me pull my shirt down over his head.

'Oh, you ticklish little girl. Ticklish?'

'No,' I pant between laughs, but he takes his mouth and blows belly farts on my stomach.

'Lymon! Lymon!' I gasp. 'Stop!' I laugh convulsively as he blows his lips against my stomach again. 'Stop!' I reach for his head and push hard.

He picks his head up suddenly. 'Oh, I'm so sorry. I got carried away there. Can I move on?' I nod, lay my head back on his hard flat pillow, and catch my breath. He raises my shirt up toward my chest.

'Oh, Lord! Oh, Lord! Is that what I think? Oh, Lord!' He clutches his heart with one hand while holding my undershirt up with the other.

'You okay?' I lift my head.

'Ohh.' He lets out a long moan. 'Ohhh . . . You have the most'—his voice splinters—'beautiful little baby nippies!' His fingers tear at his cheeks as if his face were a mask he was trying to rip off. 'So pink, and flat, and tiny and perfect!'

I stare up at the cracked wood slate ceiling. I can see the tin roof through the splits.

'Can I—can I touch?' he says between pants.

I nod and focus on the scurry of critter feet on the ceiling boards.

His fingers graze little circles around my nipples. He starts tweaking them in fast little nips as if he were grabbing pinches of salt.

I ignore the annoying sensation and his irritating squawks and gasps as I watch little clawed feet hanging over a board above our heads.

'Lymon, we gotta go soon,' I say up to the ceiling.

'Just a minute more, just, just, just . . .'

Other little tails sweep out, scurrying over to the bigger tail. I listen to the squeaks of the baby rats as they snuggle their mama.

'Lymon . . .'

'Roll over for me, sweetie, can ya, please?'

I let out a loud dissatisfied groan and roll over.

'Thank you, thank you, thank you! Now, I'm just goin' to slide off your dress here . . .' He reaches under me and works the dress down over my hips and off from around my legs. Then he starts hyperventilating so intensely I'm afraid he's going to pass out on me.

'Lymon, you wanna sit down with your head between your knees,' I say over my shoulder.

'I'm fine, I'm fine . . . just been a long time . . .'

'What about Pooh? Why didn't ya ever have a time with her?'

'Oh, she might be a young one, but she ain't no pure little girl. It's only sweet little girls, like them magazine ads, that I fancy. Okay, now, I'm gonna take down your sweet little white tights, okay?' He doesn't wait for me to answer. He just starts working his fingers around the elastic waistband.

I lay my head on my folded arms and stare at a picture of a girl pinned up to the wall six inches in front of me.

'Oh, okay, now, I'm just gonna slide them over your sweet, so sweet, tender little p-p-panties, pink p-p-pan-ties. Did Le Loup get those for ya? I bet he did, 'cause they are awful sweet.'

I nod my head against my arms and notice how the crotch and chest portions of the pinned-up girls on the wall are worn so thin you can almost see through them.

I feel him give a little tug and my tights are off.

'Oh my, oh my! I have me a pretty little princess, lying here on *my* bed in just her darlin' little pink panties! Oh my!'

'Five minutes must be up, Lymon,' I say to the girl on the wall.

'Just let me sit here and rub ya a little. I just wanna touch that pretty white soft baby skin.'

I shrug my shoulders and he eagerly sits down next to me. 'You got skin like my stepdaughter did,' he moans.

'I gotta get home, Lymon.'

'Just, just . . .' His fingers bounce off the skin on my back like a plane making a poor landing. Finally, after more hyperventilation, he begins to gently touch and caress my back, arms, and legs.

'That does feel nice, Lymon,' I say and rub at my heavy-feeling eyelids. 'Think I still have some of that drug in me.'

'Aw, you just, you just relax now.'

'That does feel good, though. Nobody has touched me for a long time,' I say into my arms.

'That's all right, sweet little thing.' He runs his other hand through my hair, stroking it like he's combing a horse mane. 'Such beautiful golden curls, my sweet thing, sweet thing,' he sings in his womanly pitched voice. I let my eyes close for a bit.

'I gotta get home,' I mutter into the mattress and fall fast asleep.

'What happened to it?' Lymon shakes me awake.

I open my eyes and wipe at the drool coming out of my mouth. 'Huh?' I look around wildly to get my bearings. It takes me a minute to remember where I am.

'Where's your private hole?' Lymon sounds slightly panicked.

'Between my cheeks of course,' I say and wipe up more drool on my arm with the edge of his pillow. I suddenly realize my panties are not on me. 'Hey, you said you weren't gonna put nothin' in me. How long I been sleeping for?'

'Where's your other hole at?' Lymon's voice isn't in that shrill chafing timbre any more and I'm grateful.

'Huh? I gotta go, Lymon.' I start to push myself up.

Lymon pushes me back down, which so surprises me I stay down. I feel him spreading my legs with his hands. His fingers probe between my legs.

'Oh, Jesus,' he says and squeezes hard between my legs.

I let out a yelp of pain.

'Oh, sweet Jesus!' he says louder. He reaches up under my belly and flips me onto my back.

He says nothing. He only stares, his face registering shock.

I slowly reach my hand down, between my legs, to my penis.

'What are you?' Lymon asks, and I see a darkness slowly replacing the shock across his face.

I don't know what to say. I feel as surprised as he is. I touch it again. It's still there, like it always is.

'What are you?!' he shouts and I jump up.

'Please just take me home,' I whisper.

'What are you?!' he screams. 'Are you the devil?! Are you a snake?! What the hell are you?!' he screams at the tops of his lungs.

'Please, Lymon, I just want to go home!' I start moving toward the door.

'You are not a little girl!' he howls and suddenly lunges for me. I leap out of the way, scramble to the doorway, and push the thin balsawood door off its hinges and run naked out of Lymon's shack.

I hear Lymon running, shrieking behind me, but he's not chasing me. I realize he's running in the direction of the diner and he's shouting for help. I run toward the trucks lined up waiting for Pooh, but then I think better of that. I spin around and around trying to decide in a panic where to go. I decide to run back to Lymon's and grab my clothes, but then I see up at the diner folks spilling out, waving what looks like flaming torches.

I run toward the bog forest.

I hear them yelling for me, calling me by every name of Satan I have ever heard, and then some I'd never heard. The pitcher plants, sundews, and bladderworts all bite at my legs and ankles and the mosquitoes are sucking me like a cherry soda. But I don't move. I stay hidden behind some huge foul-smelling skunk cabbage leaves. I peek out to see the mob carrying their torches ablazing. 'Oh God,' I cry under my breath. 'Oh my God.'

'She-Ra! She-Ra! Sarah! Sarah! She-Ra!' I make out Pooh's voice calling to me. I peek out and can see her on the edge of the forest, by herself, searching the bushes with a flashlight. I stand up and let the shaft she throws toward me catch me.

'Is that you?' she calls out in a loud whisper.

'Turn off the light,' I whisper back loudly.

She flicks off the light and I hear her stumbling through the brush. 'Where are you?'

'Here, here . . .' I guide her with my voice. I see her outline in front of me and tap her shoulder. She jumps. 'Damn!' She turns toward me and lets her eyes adjust to the crescent moonlight. 'Ugh, it stinks here!'

I become aware of the staggering urge to throw myself into her arms. I wrap my hands around myself and just let the trembling move through me.

'You're peach-pit naked,' Pooh says.

I nod at the obvious. She looks down toward my crotch, shakes her head, and starts to laugh.

'Oh, Lord!' she snickers. 'I'm sorry.' She reaches out her hand and slaps my shoulder. 'That thing looks like a fried dill pickle!' Pooh folds over with laughter.

For some reason I start laughing too, though it quickly fades into crying, but I keep my tone the same so Pooh can't tell.

'Uh,' Pooh says, wiping at her eyes, 'I'm sorry, just might as well be a second nose. It does look out of place on ya.'

'I never asked for it to be there.'

'Well, if those folks catch ya'—she points over her shoulder toward the diner—'they might oblige ya!' She lets out a little chortle.

'Can you help me, Pooh?' I grab the sleeve of her leather jacket.

'What the fuck happened?' She hits the side of my head with her palm like I had forgotten something momentous. I let go of her arm and step back. A look of surprised offense, that I thought she might hurt me, briefly bisects her face. 'You were supposed to go with Lymon to go home, not to fuck him!' she says somewhat spitefully.

'I don't know what happened . . .' I look at my bare feet slowly disappearing under the spongy mossy earth.

'What happened is you got greedy. He told everyone how you made him give you five hundred dollars!'

'Five? Two, it was two!'

'Whatever it fuckin' was! Jesus! You know what he likes. Did you forget what you are? Did you forget what you *really* are?' She hits my arm.

'You knew,' I whisper.

She hits my arm again. 'I knew you both wouldn't be able to help yourselves! Since I met you, you never get enough.' She slaps a bug on my chest. 'I knew you just couldn't say no to taking Lymon's money! I know you think too highly of yourself!' I watch the bug's flattened body oozing out on me.

'It wasn't his money.'

'So, it's his good looks?!' she snorts.

'It wasn't his money.'

'Yeah, I'm sure it wasn't. Just like I'm sure Le Loup only paid you in Barbies. How much you get off Le Loup?'

I shake my head.

'Where'd you hide all your money at? You tell me and I'll get you out of here.'

'You knew Lymon wouldn't take me home,' I say and close my eyes.

'Yeah, it's my fault, it's all my fault. I'm the one that made you make a play for Le Loup back at the Jackalope, for Le Loup, my only true love. I'm the one that convinced you to let everyone suppose you were a fuckin' saint. And I sure as shit must be the one that persuaded you to lay your lazy ass all day on a bed, performing miracles, stealing trucker dollars, and turning Le Loup into a panty-washing pedophile freak like Lymon! Now, I don't know who or for that matter what you are. And if anyone tempts somebody to believe in folk magic, you surely do, 'cause a snake'—she points between my legs—'is all I see, or ever saw.'

I exhale like I've been gut-punched.

'So you better tell me where your money is at. Otherwise, I'm going to holler like a pig stuck under a fence! See, I knew you wasn't gonna leave all your money behind too.'

'I don't know how all this happened,' I say quietly. 'I couldn't stop it. Any of it.'

'I know you hid it. I've searched all over Le Loup's for it. Where's the money?'

'And I am sorry for it. All of it.'

'Tell it to Saint Peter. Don't waste my time. Where is it?!'

I wipe the dead bug off me. 'There's two hundred in my shoe at Lymon's.'

'And the money Le Loup gave you?'

I take a deep breath. I close my eyes again and picture Sarah. I let her move within me. 'Pooh, if I tell you, you get me home. You put me on a truck going home and you'll see me leaving. I'll have no way to get that money. And it's a lot of money.'

'I'll get the money first, then I'll get you home.'

'No, Pooh. I know how you play dolls. You get me on a truck now. Then I'll tell you where the money is and you can go get it while I'm on my way home.'

'Why the fuck should I trust you to tell me where it's hid?'

''Cause I'll have no use for that money, Pooh. Like I said, I'll be gone. And 'cause I want to pay you back for helping me.'

Pooh reaches out and tugs on a chunk of her hair and absent-mindedly pulls it out. She constricts her charcoal-outlined eyes at me. 'You won't get out of here without my help.'

'Okay, then I'll burn.' I stare straight back at her. 'And believe me, I'll be in no mood then to tell you where that money is hid.'

Pooh takes a step back as if I had just hit her.

'And it is hid good.'

'I have a driver waiting all ready to take you.' She points off toward a side road that leads to the freeway. 'The deal is, as soon as you get inside his cab you tell me where it's hid at.'

'Deal.'

'But you call it your Barbies. You say, "Pooh, my Barbies are" wherever the money is at. Got it? I don't want that trucker to CB anyone about where to find no stolen loot.'

'You trust him to take me home?'

'He ain't no Lymon and he ain't no fag,' she says sarcastically. 'He loves *me*.' Pooh makes a grand sweep with her arm that results in her pointing at herself. 'He'll do as I say.'

I nod. 'Okay.'

'Okay.' She nods. 'Here.' She takes off her jacket. 'Cover that damned thing up, for God's sake.'

We climb out of the rank bushes and walk along the edge of the morose forest. A black Peterbilt is parked near the edge of the forest, near a torn-up old tar road leading to the freeway.

'I wasn't gonna let them burn ya. I knew I'd find ya in the forest,' Pooh says, patting my back. 'See, I had your escape planned.' She points to the truck.

'Thanks, Pooh,' I say, trying not to sound flat.

We walk up to the cab door. Pooh does a rhythmical knock

and my heart seethes through me, standing out in the open, waiting.

'Let yourself in, Pooh,' a deep, nondescript voice calls from inside.

'Ask him if he'll make a stop at Paymart and run in to get me some clothes. I'll pay him when I get home.'

She nods, climbs the steps of the cab, and pulls open the door. She motions me to follow her. I lean out from behind to get a glimpse of the trucker taking me home. He's hunched over a huge road map, following the little blue and red veins with his finger. He looks up at us briefly, then stares back at his map with his worn leather trucker face. The fact that he's examining a map, planning my escape, puts me at ease.

'That's who we had to come back for?' he grunts.

Pooh turns around to me, her face set in an exhortative glare. 'Where are the dolls?'

I look at the trucker. 'What did he mean by what he said?'

Pooh slaps my arm and I turn back toward her. 'Do you want to go home?' she whispers angrily.

'Yeah, this is who,' says another voice.

I feel as if I had suddenly been dipped in freezing ice water.

'The dolls,' Pooh says to me with rage under her breath.

'I took those dolls away, Pooh. You know that. Ain't fittin' play for a saint.'

I turn slowly to see the lizard-skin boots.

'It's fittin' play for sweet little girls.' Le Loup's hand reaches out and casually undoes the knot on my hip I had tied the arms of Pooh's jacket into.

'Told ya I'd find her,' Pooh says eagerly.

I watch the tie come undone and Le Loup languidly pulls the jacket covering me away.

'Which neither of ya are . . .'

'I know they got some stills hid in these hollers here.' The trucker bangs his finger on the map.

'We'll get back there. Just as soon as I take care of some trouble here,' Le Loup says.

'Should I get back to work, Le Loup?' Pooh calls out from behind me.

'I know how you love to work, Pooh. Far be it from me to keep ya from your calling.'

'I'll see ya later.' I hear Pooh turn and yank on the door handle.

'And, Pooh . . .'

'Yeah?'

'I sure hope I don't find out you were involved in any of this. I sure hope I don't find it was you that gave Lymon the idea, or helped him some . . .'

'Le Loup, I can't vouch for what Lymon or any of them jealous drunkards might tell ya.' Pooh swallows loudly. 'I just know Lymon's been begging for a poke at her'—she clears her throat—'him'—her eyebrows raise in correction—'and I guess he just had to go take it. If I'd've known, I'd've told you.'

'Get out of here, Pooh.'

I hear the door being yanked again and before I can even think about it, I say, 'I never hid any *dolls*, Pooh. There isn't any, never was.'

I hear Pooh slam the cab door behind her and stomp down the stairs.

'Gonna have to remind Pooh later about slamming those doors,' Le Loup says with a snarl.

I try to raise my eyes but can't go any higher then the edges of his boots. My hands are just dangling at my sides. I want to cover myself, but don't dare move.

For the first time in a long time, standing there, waiting to experience the wrath of Le Loup, I feel the safety of the familiar and it lends me a feeling of terrifying calm.

'Kent, drive over to my place,' Le Loup says without moving.

'Sure thing.' I hear the map being folded up, and even though it is now clear he wasn't using it to plot our course to my home, I feel a sickening sense of loss.

The truck pulls out and drives slowly to Le Loup's. I feel his stare boring into me. My body bounces and wobbles with the truck and I steady myself now and again by reaching for the passenger seat, but my eyes stay down.

When the truck stops, Le Loup says the first words he's said directly to me, 'Get out.'

I turn, pull the door open, and climb down.

Le Loup says some words to Kent, then drops down behind me. Wordlessly he walks to the barn door and opens it. I follow him into the stale cool inside.

The muscles in his back seem to loosen and collapse some as he walks into his house and we are alone together.

I want to say something. Something that will explain everything, fix everything. If I were Sarah I would know what to say and how to say it. She always knows what to say.

For the first time I look him in the face. His face twitches slightly as my eyes meet his, as if a cold wind had suddenly hit his face. He opens his mouth to say something, but closes it again.

I sense a longing in his look, and I want to say the right thing to capture it and hold it. He turns from me and drags a wood stool into the middle of the room.

'Sit,' he says peacefully.

I move over to the chair and climb up onto it. I let my hands fall into my lap, concealing myself. Le Loup gently takes my hands, picks them up, and drops them to my sides.

I watch him reach down into his boot. He takes out something, which he fumbles with in his hands.

'It has to be this way,' he says and opens a long switchblade.

And with a cold inert awareness, I realize what I took for longing was really the look of mourning on Le Loup's face.

I suddenly can't breathe and begin to pant. I shake my head no. And I recognize his face. It was a face he never had for me, but for the lizards he would drag into his room to discipline. And now I realize his face usually contained a yielding affection when he dealt with me. The clenched rage set of his face is directed completely at me now, and it feels like staring into the pit of death. I try to say something, anything, but the words are stuck well beneath my larynx. He moves so he is standing between my parted legs.

'Good-bye, Sarah,' he says, and raises the blade above me. I see a whirl of it flash by, feel a sharp cut, followed by a vague awareness of some part of me falling to the ground.

I am lying on the floor. Afternoon light is hitting my face in long bright bars. I feel an ache, a fierce piercing ache somewhere. My hand feels damp. I raise it to my eyes and see blood. Everything dissolves to black.

'Get up.' I feel a sharp poking at my side. 'Wake up.' I open my eyes to see Le Loup standing in a haze above me. I'm aware of voices coming from outside. I tilt my head to see the tempered evening light streaming in.

'Am I almost dead?' I whisper.

'Get up!' Le Loup's foot bangs into my side harder.

I am amazed that I am able to push myself up onto my elbows and, after more prods from Le Loup's boot, to sit up. I avoid looking down, between my legs. I am vaguely aware of crimson streaks on my body. My head throbs and aches like a million paper cuts.

I feel beyond tears.

The thought passes through my mind to grasp on to his legs and beg for . . . for something. Just to latch on and not let go no matter how hard he kicks.

'Get up!' Le Loup reaches down, grabs me by my arm and hauls me to my feet.

I am further astonished I can stand, let alone walk, as he half drags me toward the bathroom.

He kicks open the door and pulls me in with him. This is where he will finish me off. I am probably bleeding too much, so the tub would work better for . . .

'Look!' he says.

I twist my head from the tub to look at him.

'Look!' He's staring straight ahead and he jabs me to do the same.

I turn my head to look at him looking at me in the mirror. It's a window-frame mirror, lit by a border of round lightbulbs, the kind of mirror you would find in a star's dressing room. I've stood in front of this mirror many times attempting the effortless fluid motions with which Sarah could wink an eye, throw a kiss, and toss her hair, all at the same time.

'Look!' Le Loup prods me hard.

I turn my head and, in the mirror's reflection, I see someone standing next to Le Loup. Someone I don't recognize. The person's hair has been sliced off. Lacerations and blood streaks mar the virginal whiteness of the scalp. There is one long gold curly lock left, hanging in the front like a unicorn's limp horn. Le Loup, staring in the mirror, reaches for it. He unfurls it like he's straightening a spring coil. His switchblade raises in the air and rains down in a fast vicious swoop. Like a bird piercing the water's surface to snatch up its prey, the blade scrapes into the scalp to cut loose the remaining tassel of hair. Le Loup clenches the lock in his fist above his head.

A trickle of blood runs over the bare scalp, dribbles down the forehead, spreading at the eyebrows, to finally gather into one fine ruby droplet. I watch the droplet, like a diamond-shaped tear, loosen and fall with a tiny splash into an eye.

My eye.

I blink at the droplet and it seeps around my socket, turning the white into a runny pink.

I hear a laugh, low and guttural at first. Then I realize it's a war whoop. I turn to see Le Loup pumping his fist in the air over my head, his mouth protracted into a victory cry. He suddenly grabs me with his other arm and pulls me out of the bathroom. The voices outside are louder, extending into a tenacious grumble.

We move past the stool I had been sitting on, and I see scattered around it, like tinsel fallen off a Christmas tree, the rest of my hair.

He pulls me to the barn's door and unlocks it. Before he opens it, he steps behind me, pulls my arms in back of me and binds my wrists together.

'You stay here,' he says, moving me to lean against a wall next to the closed door. The fact that he doesn't even bother to remind me to not even think about escaping makes me feel all the more forfeited and discarded.

Le Loup throws open the barn door. I hear his boots clicking onto the wood deck and stopping there. The voices of what sounds like a modest crowd quickly hush.

I lean back against the wall and let my body sink to the floor.

There is only silence from outside. Finally, through the partially open door, I hear Le Loup striking a match against the

wood porch rail. It's so silent I can even make out his first in-
halation and exhalation. I smell smoke wafting in. It's not the
warm tobacco puffs from a cigarette, but a sooty-wood petroleum
burn from lit torches. I picture the stack of wood they have piled
around a wood stake. Like Joan of Arc, I will go up in a blaze of
flames. I imagine Sarah hearing the news that I died a lot-lizard
martyr and know that besides being insanely heartbroken at my
loss, she'll be impressed if not more than a little jealous.

After what must be a half-dozen slow leisurely drags, Le Loup
clears his throat.

'I want to thank all you for coming out on such a pleasant
autumn evening.' Le Loup's voice is serene, but there is clearly a
malevolent layer within his tone.

'Been a lot of excitement around here lately, from what I understand.' For the first time since Le Loup appeared, the crowd
breaks its silence with a low murmur of agreement.

'I've heard there's been talk of black magic.' Again the throng
assents enthusiastically.

'Accusations of metamorphosis, charges of chicanery, and'—
Le Loup's boots stop pacing—'crimes against nature.' Before the
crowd can respond, Le Loup continues, 'I also know that when
the money was rolling in, there was a whole mess of talk about
miracles, saints, and a host of testifying on the glories and rev-
elations of Jesus.' His voice takes on the melodious character of
a call-and-response tent-show preacher, though nobody calls a
thing in response.

'Mmmm, the money was rolling and rolling in and I don't believe I overheard any discussions of fire and its possible use on *my*
home or *my* property, back then. But perhaps I'm wrong.' I hear
the crowd shift uncomfortably. 'Is there anyone here that would
like to enlighten me on the benefits of fire and its many uses?'
Again I hear more nervous shuffling. 'Are y'all sure? 'Cause I am

here willing to benefit from your wisdom and knowledge!' I hear
him start to move again. 'Now, I'm very concerned about this
black snake within our midst. I'm burdened with worry over how
severely damaged you all have been by this black snake.' I hear
Le Loup drag one of the porch chairs over. 'So I'm just going to
sit here and I want you to feel free to come on up here and tell me
how you personally suffered. C'mon, y'all! I know you ain't shy.
Stella?' I recognize Stella's dry cough in response to Le Loup's
calling upon her. 'Petunia? Now I know the fleecin' you gave to
all them visiting Yanks, and various others that made themselves
a pilgrimage here, could not compare to the loss y'all incurred on
those smart little makeup compacts and those television-friendly
supplementary wardrobes. I must agree, it does sound like the
plain work of The Archfiend to me.' Stella's cough sounds more
like a plea for invisibility than an actual cough. 'So, c'mon up,
Stella! Petunia! C'mon! Aww, don't tell me you're gettin' demure
on me. And what about you, Mary Grace?' Le Loup's chair gives
a turning scrape. 'Now, I heard rumors, and I never put much
faith in rumors, that you and all the crew at the diner sold potato
crèches to a fair number of our recent visitors. Now, I understand
you have a number of sacks left that're growing eyes faster than
a blind man in a strip joint. Well, that is quite a financial hit for
you and no doubt the work of a monarch of hell!' I hear Mary
Grace whispering something. 'Ya know I won't take no for an
answer!' Le Loup says with sardonic hospitality. 'C'mon up! I'm
tellin' y'all that the black snake is in there now!' He stomps his
foot. 'Bring ya torches and toss them in! C'mon! Won't none of
you?' My heart picks up some after his invitation to incinerate
me, and I strain to hear any movements toward him being taken
up on his offer. Le Loup rises to his feet. 'Lymon!' he says as
if Lymon were a long-lost relation. 'Lymon! Take one of those
blazes and burn this evil thing out my house, will ya?' Le Loup

moves toward the barn door. 'That li'l girl . . .' He says the last word with proficient sarcasm. 'She gave ya quite a scare there, didn't she?' Le Loup slaps the barn door. 'You were just trying to molest a sweet little thing while her daddy was away and things just didn't work out, is what I heard. That's awful, just awful, and I am truly sorry.' I can see Le Loup's shadow head shaking back and forth. 'What say ya, Lymon? Hmm?'

There's a long pause of absolute silence.

'Any of ya?' Only crickets and a far-off wolf howling answer.

'Well, I got something to tell you.' Before I can blink, Le Loup comes bursting through the door and grabs me up. He hauls me to the door and out onto the porch.

A collective gasp ripples through the crowd. I stare at my bare feet that strike me as looking like some bizarre manifestation against the ordinary gray of the wood beneath them.

'I'd like you all to meet . . .' Le Loup pauses, then pushes my chin up with his hand. 'Sam.' It's so quiet you can here the crackle of the torches. I look over the heads and flames to focus on the surrounding hills.

'Now, since I take it none of you have decided to burn this' — he jerks my arm and I take an unbalanced step forward — 'black snake . . . then I take it we can all just finish going about our business.' Lit by a sliver of moon, the wind's aimless stirrings make it seem as if invisible creatures were romping through the grassy plateaux.

'Now, if any of y'all wanna visit with Sam here, he'll be workin' over at Stacey's lot. You can make your appointments with Stacey or me if you want to book some time. You got that, Lymon?' There's a subdued current of forced laughter, which is quickly swallowed into an awful silence of nighttime bog noises.

From the corner of my eye, I see Le Loup scanning the group. 'All right, then . . . you all have a nice night.'

With that, Le Loup turns and walks us back inside. The warmth of inside almost hurts, as I defrost the cold and terror that I must've been feeling, because it is quite some time before I stop shaking.

'Put those on.' Le Loup points to some folded-up jeans, a shirt, and a worn pair of sneakers. 'Pooh's old things ought to fit,' he says and goes to the kitchen, sits with a dark sigh, and pours himself a drink into one of Pooh's jam-jelly jars.

It's been a long time since I've worn jeans and I slide my feet into the legs slowly, as if there might be a hidden danger lurking inside. As I pull up the jeans, I'm surprised by my mouth being pulled down, by some unseen force, into a trembling half moon. As I pull up the fly it sticks, no matter how hard I tug. And suddenly the inability to take in air begins. It's as if all the oxygen were sucked out of the room and only the stuck cry in my chest could release it.

'Get those clothes on,' Le Loup calls from behind the kitchen counter.

From a draft, a little dust tumbleweed comes rolling toward me. As it crosses my foot I realize it is a clump of my shorn golden hair. And it's as if I were suddenly injected with a poison. It takes hold in my fingers. I watch them spread apart and stiffen. Then my legs lose their connective tissue and the ability to hold me standing. I crumble over onto my knees. As they hit the floor, it's as if something is knocked loose and a long loud sob escapes me.

'What the fuck are you doing?!' Le Loup yells and moves to his feet.

Another sob racks my body, and I can only bow over under its crushing weight.

'Get those damn clothes on!' Le Loup stomps next to me. 'Now!'

I gasp for air before the next wave hits me.

'Goddamn you!' Le Loup shouts. I manage to turn my head toward him as he pulls back his arm holding the glass. 'Goddamn you!' he screams and pulls back even farther, like it's a football aimed for my head. He wails as he releases the jar and it flies in an arc till it smashes a good five feet from my person. 'Goddamn you!' he howls and stalks out of the barn, slamming the door behind him.

I work the lot behind the old outhouses, hidden by a tangle of laurel breaks, and reached by a dusty dirt road. In connected broken-down trailers waiting for a good storm to finish them off, six other lizards live here too. All males. Stacey, a bald, obese, and, as rumor has it, former truck driver, with over-tweezed eyebrows, is the house daddy. He sits in a La-Z-Boy recliner that's the indistinct color of fingernail dirt all day and half the night, booking his boys dates over the CB, watching satellite feeds of soap operas from every country in the world, even though he speaks only English, but by conditioning knows just when to laugh, cry, or bite his nails in worry. Lately he had been admiring one of the villainesses on a soap from Portugal and had ordered a Portuguese home-language course so he could learn to become verbally as caustic yet quick-witted as her facial expressions implied she was.

All his boys sleep in logger-camp-style bunkbeds in back. I'm the youngest, but nobody either hassles me or takes me under their wing. I am tolerated with a vaguely benign indifference.

Two of the lizards are hopeless sugar-whiskey drunks, working enough to buy the inflatedly priced flasks Stacey sells them. The other two are brokenhearted, left at Three Crutches by their former trucker lovers, and live only to drown their sorrows in inhaled bags of glue and the assorted solvents Stacey also sells to them with a significant markup. Stacey's prices are so high that everyone ends up taking out loans from him and, before they know it, racking up a substantial debt. So, even if anyone fancies leaving, until they pay up, they ain't going nowhere.

The boy closest to my age is a thief, finally caught trying to make it out the window of Three Crutches with the entire cash register and ten cans of liver mush. Like the rest, and me, he is indentured here until the debt is paid.

Just like firemen we are on call 24/7, though it never gets too busy. Mostly everyone sleeps off their highs or sits on red metal folding chairs watching Stacey's soaps.

The johns that mostly visit Stacey's goodbuddy lizards are truckers too poor to afford the more expensive mare lizards in the main lot, and are too horny or drunk to care.

There is nothing delicate or gentle in their lovin'. Before Stacey sends me out on a little brother seatcover date, I buy off of one of the others a few gulps or whiffs, enough to get me through. I pay them with the tips I don't turn over to Stacey like I'm supposed to. He's caught me a few times and whipped me bad, but not bad enough to make me try to do those dates straight.

The johns don't talk, don't hardly look at me. They handle me rough, like a steering wheel they have to bully through a tight turn. They blame me if they're too drunk and they blame me if they ain't drunk enough. They mostly never ever tip and it took me a few weeks to break my old training from Glad's of politely loitering until they hand over a tip. Also cost me a good number of black eyes and a few chips on my teeth. Eventually I figured out why I used to see those lizards with no pimps to protect them, leaping out of cabs like shots out of a cannon. When these tricks get done it's best to haul out fast, 'cause some suddenly remember you're just professional beaver, faggot beaver at that.

They have to beat us pretty good for Stacey to even bother to tell Le Loup about it. Stacey just hands over the key to the first aid kit and doesn't mind you drinking up the ninety weight tucked in there.

The gay drivers usually send me back, telling me I'm a road runt and they're looking for a man. The dates I look forward to are the Lavender Larry drivers, the men who talk to me the way Lymon did when he fancied me a girl. Their hands quiver the same way, they touch real gentle, and talk of love. They're the only ones I ever get a chance to practice developing my second sight on, but because they all want the same thing, there's not much for me to practice with.

They always promise to come back for me on their return run. They enchant me with intricate tales on how they will rescue and adopt me as their son. After devotedly watching for a couple of them, diligently scanning the CB for a sign or signal all winter only to watch the snow thaw and still be waiting, I now stop any Larry from uttering a word of promises. I let them kiss my hand goodbye, assure them I don't need or want them to rescue me, but I do look forward to their return. I stuff half their tip in my underwear and the other in my pocket for Stacey to snatch.

We're not permitted to go to the diner, so I haven't seen any of the diner folks in a long time. We eat cans of microwaved SpaghettiOs and pepperoni rolls from Clarksburg. Haven't even seen Le Loup since the day he left me here. I watch for him, though. I watch the road from my private perch on top of the old outhouses, where I get a clear view of the freeway. Every now and then I see his purple Trans Am heading toward us and I pray this'll be the time he'll turn down the dusty dirt road. He'll tell me I've repaid my debt and I am free to leave. As a matter of fact he'll take me home himself. But his car always passes by without even slowing.

The Thief tried to escape once. But there are only two ways out. Through the bogs is one way, and no one has ever heard of anything but dead bodies being hauled out on the other side Then there's the freeway. The forest runs too thick with untraversable laurel brakes on either side of the road, so any hitchhiker is forced to walk on the black tar pavement of the road itself. Wouldn't be but ten minutes at the outside till Stacey overhears the talk on the CB about some foot tourist on the highway and before he asks for someone to lay an eye out as to what this road bird might look like. Usually somebody just recognizes one of Stacey's lizards and lets him know he's got a stray on the loose. Trying to get a trick to drive you out is worse. No matter how many Kentucky apple-fried pies Stacey has consumed, no matter if as a result he appears as glassy-eyed and catatonic as one of the glue sniffers, he has a superhuman knack for keeping track of all his boy's dates and how long they've been gone. He has a talent for knowing when one of his is going to try to ride his way out. That truck would hardly get out onto the highway when the old air-raid siren up at the diner would sound. It was well known in the trucker community: Le Loup's lizards were not to be taken out on loan. Any trucker snared trying got no sympathy for his broken bones and other assorted injuries. Dumber than a fence post and deserving whatever came his way, is what other truckers said about those who tried to sneak off with a lizard. The only lizards that usually ever have the balls to attempt it are the ones out of supplies, hoping to make their own glue or liquor run and cut Stacey out of the loop. They never get far, and they fare far from well after getting caught. I heard that the escaping thief had eagerly jumped into the purple Trans Am that had pulled over to pick him up. I heard he told the driver to step on it and he'd pay him well. I heard they drove a good five miles before The Thief looked over to see it was Le Loup himself driving, waiting to see how long it would take for The Thief to notice.

It was two months before anyone saw him again. And he

still walks with a wobble to his hips, and his face, like a washed-out berry pie stain, still bears the remnants of the lesson he was taught.

My only hope has been the one Lavender Larry I truly trusted. I hushed his lips before he could swear to save me. I slipped him a note with the name Glading Grateful ETC . . . of The Doves Diner. 'Please call and tell him I am stuck here,' I said, as I tucked the folded paper into his chest pocket and pressed it with my hand, over his heart.

From my perch I watch, hoping one day I'll see Glad rolling in. I'm pretty sure he'd buy me back if he knew where I was. I'm even pretty sure he'd cross the Cheat for me. It'd been months, but maybe Glad was waiting for the thaw.

Finally one spring day, sitting up on my roost, I see a familiar figure marching through the grassy sods toward me. I squint and try to make out who. It's the walk, low to the ground but with a tough swagger. I leap down and run toward it, only to slow to a halt when I see it's Pooh. She waves her arms and smiles as if we had had a tea party only yesterday. I want to turn and show her my back, just walk away, but seeing her fills me with hope for some reason.

'Hey!' Pooh whisper-shouts at me. 'I heard I could find ya here.' She positively sparkles in a red satin jumpsuit with knee-high boots and her hair done like a Nashville country star.

'Jesus, Pooh! You look like a movie star!' I say when she gets close enough.

'And you . . .' She takes a step back. 'No offense, but you look like shit. I'd've thought your long curls would've done been grown back by now!' She runs her hand over my crew-cut head.

I jerk my head away from her touch without thinking. A look of surprise and then something that resembles a mix of annoyance and hurt passes over her face as she leaves her hand suspended in the air.

I clear my throat. 'I'm not allowed to grow my hair in.' I look at her boots, lizard skin like Le Loup's.

'You're kidding me?!' She lowers her hand.

'No. Le Loup's orders. Stacey buzzes me himself every ten days on the dot.'

Pooh looks at me, shakes, then turns her head and spits. 'Well, funny you should say I look like a movie star, 'cause I am on my way to Hollywood!'

I squint at her. 'Are you for real? Hollywood?' She nods. 'Le Loup is just lettin' you go?'

'A famous Hollywood agent heard of my fame, all the way out there in California, and he came here himself and you might as well have buttered his butt and called him a biscuit, 'cause he was mine right from the get-go!' Pooh slaps her leg in laughter.

'How'd you pull that off?'

'Used my second sight to know all he wanted was to be wrapped in diapers, nursed with a bottle, and burped like an armbaby. He had never told a being in this world, bless his poor tortured soul, but I knew!'

'Damn . . .' I shake my head in impressed jealousy.

'He bought me from Le Loup and now we're leaving to begin on my film career! He says anyone with my gifts will have no problem convincing all the world's famous directors and them studio heads of my inspiring and advantageous talent.'

'Well, Pooh, congratulations. I wish you well. If you came to gloat, well, I hope it makes ya feel all the better. I'll make ya feel even more better by asking you if I could have your old flask as a souvenir.'

'No, I actually . . .'

'And I'll further make your day by asking, beggin' if you fancy, if you could find a way to fill it with that rotgut you swigged day and night.'

Pooh takes my arm. 'Sarah . . .'

Hearing my mother's name spoken out loud by someone else combined with a gentle touch unsteadies me. I grab Pooh back and hold on.

'I actually came here to reattach some heads and limbs,' she says softly.

We stand quietly watching a red-spotted newt totter over my worn sneakers.

'Here.' She lets go of me and reaches under her pant-suit blouse. She slowly works a leather thong from around her neck. She carefully removes it, mindful not to mess her hair.

'This is yours.' She holds out my raccoon penis bone.

I stare at it lying there in Pooh's hand and it looks to me like an artifact from some lost civilization. I start laughing.

'What?' Pooh says, starting to laugh herself in contagion.

I laugh so hard I can't speak. Finally I catch some breath, 'Ya know, Pooh, you were right about me.' I laugh some more. 'I am greedy! I wanted a bigger fuckin' bone, the hugest fuckin' bone, and . . .' I lift the necklace out of her hand and hold it up. 'That's what got me where the fuck I am today!'

'Well,' she starts.

'So if you think giving me my bone back is reattaching any limbs . . .' I stuff it into my pocket. 'To be honest, it'd be way more than useful to have a jug of white lightning. Fuck, I'd even take Sterno poured through Wonder bread!'

'I don't have any of that no more,' she says softly.

'Well, then.' I reach out my hand to shake hers. She gives me her hand limply and I shake it hard for the both of us. 'Well, then you have yourself a great time out there in Hollywood! I'm a busy boy.' I say the last word with corrosive spite. 'Got dicks to suck and seats to bend over!' I turn and start to walk away. 'So you don't mind if I excuse myself.'

'Sarah!' she calls.

I make fists and force myself to keep walking.

'Sarah!' I hear her start to run after me, and I start to run away. I move through the glade as fast as I can. I look over my shoulder briefly and see Pooh still chasing me. I don't know why I'm running. I only know I have to. I get to the edge of a steep bank. I sprint down it, hopping over the low shrubs of groundberry, St. John's wort, and bulrushes.

'Sarah! Wait!'

I turn my head again and trip over a blueberry bush. 'Fuck!' I tumble down the embankment and land in the moss-covered bog shallow. 'Fuck!' I flail at the cranberry and cotton grass catching my limbs.

Pooh scurries down the bank toward me. 'Here, gimme your hand.' She stands panting over me, reaching out her hand.

I grab it and with all my might pull her in.

I watch her tumble like a gymnast doing floor exercises till she lands with a big splash not far from me.

'Jesus! Fuck!' She rises and spits out a green mat of water.

I nod, seeing she's just fine, and start to pull myself out. All of a sudden I'm pulled backward, as she grabs hold of my leg and jerks me back down.

Then we're rolling around in the water, not really fighting, just struggling against each other to escape.

'It ain't all my fault all what happened to you!' Pooh pants between splashes.

'I'd fuckin' be home now if you didn't hand fuckin' deliver me to Le Loup!' I shout and push away from her.

'I know!' she yells in my ear. 'That's why I called Glad!'

I keep battling her until her words register. 'What'd you say?'

She stands up in the water and knocks the moss off her. 'I said I called Glad.'

'You did what?' I say, still feeling like I'm hearing words too dear to be actually uttered.

'Fuck! You really ruined my new outfit. Well at least my man's rich, so it won't matter none.'

'Don't fuck with me, Pooh.' I stand up next to her, and realize in the time since I've seen her last, I've grown taller than her.

'I called Glad.' She suddenly lurches down to the water and I grab her arm, thinking she's slipped. 'Thanks,' she says, and I see she was just reaching for something floating on the moss waterbed. 'This . . .' Pooh says and scoops out the coon bone necklace. 'It wasn't hard to find out what this means . . . I knew,' she says and hands the necklace back to me. 'I knew what it really meant.'

'You—you called Glad?'

'Look, I tried to get my agent to buy you out, but Le Loup wouldn't sell. Not even for a fuckload of bucks. It's a pride thing with him. A revenge thing. I think that's why Le Loup and I aren't no good with each other. We're just too pigheaded and vengeful!'

'He wouldn't sell me?'

'Nope. And he got offered a lot. And I know money means more to him than love, but I guess not more than revenge for his broken heart.'

'Fuck! What did Glad say?!' I grab on to her arm.

'He said he'd been looking for you, *Cherry Vanilla*.' She says my old Doves name with a laugh. 'He heard lots of crazy rumors, but never could track you down. Said the truth of it was crazier than any rumors he had heard.'

'Did he say anything about Sarah?'

'I just tole you what he said about you.'

'No, my mom. Sarah is my mom.'

'Sarah's your mom's name? Well, I sure wouldn't use my mom's name if I was going to try on being a saint!' she snorts.

'I didn't mean to. It just happened.' I flap my arms in exasperation. 'What did he say about her?'

Pooh shakes her head. 'Nothin'. He didn't say nothin' about her. But he knows Le Loup. So that's one good thing I did! I saved your life by not telling Le Loup you were one of Glad's, 'cause there ain't no love lost between them two!'

I nod, hungry to hear more.

'He knows trying to buy you ain't gonna work, so he's gonna send a truck.'

'He's gonna rescue me?!' I hit Pooh's arm in excitement.

'I don't think it'll be him. He says he'll never cross the Cheat. But he's sending somebody.'

'When? What should I do? What do I look for?' I grab her with both arms.

'Look.' Pooh grabs me back. 'All he says is sit tight. Just sit tight is what he said. That's it. He didn't say who, what, when, where, or the fuck how. Just sit tight! Now I gotta get changed and get out of here, because I wouldn't put it past Le Loup to go back on the deal!'

Pooh and I make our way out of the bog and up the bank.

'Sorry 'bout your clothes, Pooh.' I try wiping some of the moss off her.

'It ain't no problem. But you better get changed so Stacey don't take the birch to you thinking you tried to make a run for it.'

'Yeah, no shit.'

Pooh takes a step away from me and looks me up and down. 'Well, you sure ain't no Shirley Temple no more.'

I look her up and down likewise. 'And you sure ain't such a badass no more.'

We don't say anything for a little bit, just look at each other.

'I'll look you up at Glad's when I get settled in Hollywood.'

'I'm gonna come visit you!' I say in mock threat. 'Get me in them pictures too!' I laugh.

She puts out her hand to shake, I shake it, and somehow we pull into a hug.

'You're gonna have to pay if you're gonna try to feel me up,' Pooh whispers in my ear.

'Ain't nothing to feel,' I whisper back.

We hold each other for a while, just listening to our breaths' discordant rhythms.

We slowly release our embrace.

'Wish I'd seen Lymon's face, I'll tell ya that!' she laughs.

'I can't say it was worth it, but it was a sight.'

'Well, you must've got him fired up something fierce, 'cause he's back in the penitentiary.'

'Why?'

'Oh, he was so, umm, inspired? He took himself into town and tried to pick up a sweet little thing, who turned out to be the sheriff's one and only daughter. He still had his probation on, so he ain't gonna be seeing no natural light till Armageddon day.'

I shrug and Pooh shrugs.

'Well, thanks, Pooh.'

Pooh nods and starts to walk away. 'Le Loup really only paid you in Barbies?' she asks without turning.

'God's truth.'

'That man is slicker than cum on gold teeth.' She keeps walking.

'Sit tight,' I say.

'Yeah.' She waves and disappears into the grasses.

I resume my vigilant habits, scanning the CB and becoming observant of every new truck that pulls in. I even watch the night sky and study the habits of the various mammals, amphibians, birds, and reptiles in the area, knowing that Glad might use any manner of Choctaw magic to send me a signal.

I quit drinking and huffing, which gets me sick for a week, but I get through it.

A month passes and, as we move into summer, the wild aza leas, mountain laurel, trillium, and other blooming flowers put on a dazzling display. I feel awakened to every minute nuance of the earth and all those around me. Even my tricks notice a difference.

I hand over all my tips that even the drunk truckers start giving me.

'Well, you sure are movin' about like ya feet are on fire and ya ass is catchin',' Stacey comments as I sit between his legs while he shaves my head.

I nod and suppress a smile.

After over a month of no discernible indications of rescue, though, an insidious thought worms its way into my thoughts.

Maybe Pooh hadn't called Glad.

She had again inquired about how Le Loup had paid me. Maybe she was just trying to find out if there really was hidden money somewhere.

Pooh might've called but could have told Glad I wasn't here any more.

The more I thought about it, the more I went over and over everything she said, the more I could come to only one conclusion: Pooh had made it up.

Why wouldn't Glad send someone right away? Sit tight?! What is that? Glad would've had instructions, a plan, a strategy. Why didn't Glad say anything about Sarah? He would've at least mentioned her, told Pooh how worried she's been, something!

She fuckin' made it up,

Maybe Glad and Le Loup do hate each other. Maybe she did tell Le Loup I was once one of Glad's. Killing me wouldn't be much worse!

Every day I bargain to hold on to my hope. I make deals with myself, like if there is no signal from Glad today, I will accept Pooh was short of the truth. And every day I usually find at least five to twenty different portents of imminent rescue.

Stacey had to move his TV, CB, and La-Z-Boy outside because it had become so stifling hot inside it caused sweat to pour off him in such copious amounts that a small flood has leaked through the cracked trailer floor and down to the foundation. His sweat is such a heady mix of sugar, lard, and flour it is like a Pied Piper's call to all voles, shrews, raccoons, moles, mice, squirrels, jumping mice, rabbits, and weasels living beneath the trailer. They all came streaming out one day in search of the sweet odoriferous source. But there was a lone bat that also swooped in to join the frenzied rodents, and finding nothing particularly appealing inside, perched itself on Stacey's La-Z-Boy and watched the tortuous Brazilian soaps with the rest of us. That bat, I recognized as a signal from Glad and made preparations for my rescue.

I heard that a white-tailed deer had mounted and impregnated one of the lizards in the main lot while she was on her way to the diner. Little deer hooves were said to be clearly visible through her swollen belly. I kept to myself that I knew that had to be Choctaw magic at work and clearly was a signal to me.

One of the huffers suddenly possessed an enchanted can of shoe glue. No matter how much he poured out and inhaled, the can stayed full. I had to keep myself from letting him know he had Glading Grateful ETC . . . to thank for the miracle and not Allah, who he decided was responsible and so, consequently, he transformed into an austere practicing Muslim.

But even with all those evident confirmations that any day liberation was impending, Glad, or anyone else from The Doves, came nowhere near the vicinity of Three Crutches.

After almost two months of thousands of signs, gestures, and indications, I finally, over a stolen trucker's flask of 150 proof, accept that Pooh had in fact lied

I sit on top of my outhouse perch and raise the silver flask in a toast to Pooh. 'Here's to decapitating Barbies!' I take a big gulp and force myself to swallow. I make another toast. 'To Sarah.' A few more swigs and I lay myself down and pass out under the heavy expanse of the night.

I pursue inhaling intoxicants and drink moonshine with the tenacity of a cornered rat. To fund my increasing habit I do as many tricks as I can and steal as many wallets as I dare. Stacey tolerates my thefts with an indulgent sternness. Whenever a trucker comes raging that I'd stolen his wallet, Stacey makes a show of bellowing nonsense in Portuguese and stomps into the back to retrieve the stolen wallet. As he hands back the wallet, he always apologizes profusely for all the money being emptied out, and always offers to call in the sheriff. The truckers always understandably decline his offer, take their hollow wallets, and sulk off.

Stacey keeps the cash and hands over substances that leave me barely aware of my breath.

After summer harvests start winding down, before the winter coal shipments pick up, business gets slow. Truckers take their vacations and get to know their families again. Sometimes I go days without a rig to climb into. I have enough credit for Stacey to keep me supplied, but I miss having my dates. The other boys always talk about having to get high to help them do and then forget their tricks. But I'm pathetically aware, now I get high to fill the time between tricks. Because, no matter how rough or tough the trucker, that point of soundlessness, that instant before they are spent, is the sweetest contact anyone could ever have with anybody. I hold those moments—the tobacco and grease-stained hand lovingly caressing my throat, the lips parted in silent ecstasy, kissing my forehead like a parent placing a goodnight kiss—I replay them in slow motion as if they took place with the prolonged consumed movements of someone running under water.

As fall settles in, with hardly any trucker dates for distraction, I wrap myself deep into a narcotic cocoon, until I can hardly rise out of bed even when there is a trick to turn.

Stacey finds me in bed. 'I've put in a call for Le Loup to come deal with you,' he says, mopping his rotund face with his yellowed undershirt while shaking the switch.

'Okay,' I say, not moving from my top bunk, where I lie, watching the ceiling spiders pluck their multicolored webs like harps.

'I'm not givin' myself any more blisters from whippin' you,' Stacey says in disgust. 'You're useless as hen shit on a pump handle.' He breaks the thin birch stick in two and heads back outside to his La-Z-Boy. 'Let Le Loup discipline you himself.'

'Okay,' I say and pass out in a wallpaper-glue haze.

'He wants you, just you!' The Thief is shaking me awake.

I keep my eyes closed and swallow a big green burp. 'What?' I mumble.

'He wants you.'

'Le Loup wants me?' I murmur, and try to pull myself up. I force open my eyes. The idea of Le Loup wanting me, even if it is to break every bone in my body, is somehow very comforting.

'You should get out there . . ' The Thief lends me a hand as he yanks me up.

I shakily lower myself off the bunk. I check my flask, vaguely remembering it being empty. 'Thief, loan me a lit.' I feel the sickening potency of withdrawal asserting itself.

'If I had somethin', be long gone. You better get out there. You're wanted bad.'

'Well, nice knowing ya,' I say sincerely. I am resigned with an indifference to the likelihood that Le Loup is going to kill me. If I'm lucky, at the least, do me great bodily damage.

'Princess!' Thief says disparagingly.

'I was once,' I say and steady myself with one hand as I walk away, sore from Stacey's thrashings, too much bed rest, and a steady diet of intoxicants.

When I get outside to Stacey, he actually looks up from his soaps. The flashing reds and blues from the screen fill in the pockmarks on his face, making them look like overflowing volcanoes.

'So! You decided to get your free-ride ass out of bed? What, you tired of pressing sheets?'

'Where is he?' I look around for Le Loup's Trans Am.

'Over there,' he says and points to our lot, hidden behind a small clump of one-sided, wind-stunted red spruce and contorted yellow birch.

'Stacey, lemme owe you for a few shots?' I grab his meaty arm, hold out my empty flask, and try my once irresistible wide-eyed virginal look, but judging by the way he gapes back at me, I know I merely look bug-eyed and desperate. 'Don't make me face him empty!'

Stacey shakes my arm off his and slaps the flask out of my hand. 'Get your ass outta here 'fore I tar it out more for you!'

'Please!' I am suddenly aware of feeling a very old familiar dread. 'I can't go without! Please! I've got the sickness!'

Stacey lets out a long sigh followed by an even louder passing of wind. 'Don't think this ain't gonna add to your bill with Le Loup!' he says, shaking the massive key ring he always wears. He pulls it out on its chain, unlocks a huge box next to his chair, and rummages around and brings up a clay jug. He retrieves my flask. I lick my lips as I watch him fill it. A viscerally clear recollection of Sarah's face holding a similar expression while a bartender would fill her glass pops into my consciousness.

He barely finishes pouring by the time I get the flask to my lips.

'Well, now you're wetter than deer guts on a stick shift. Get your ass out there!' Stacey reaches for the broken switch and tosses it at me.

'Thanks, Stace. I'll pay ya back next lifetime,' I say sincerely.

'You'll pay me back a lot sooner than that! Now get!'

I head into the pathetic thatch of trees, having to stop every ten steps to keep my trajectory headed in the general vicinity of the lot. When I get to the clearing, I don't see the purple shiny Trans Am I had prepared myself for. Just a truck similar to the one Pooh had led me to when she turned me over to Le Loup.

I turn my face straight up toward the atmosphere as I walk toward my fate. It's one of those eerie black skies that has white cloud streaks that look like teeth marks.

I stumble over a raised chunk of roadway and fly, for what feels like a good ten minutes, over the mass, skidding on my hands and knees as if stealing home.

I lie there. I consider never getting up. Never moving. Just becoming one with the asphalt. I raise my head to look at the truck. It's just sitting there, like a truck would in any lot. I try to distinguish something about the truck that might give me a clue as to what exactly Le Loup is going to do to me. The truck definitely has a somber air to it, similar to a hearse, I decide.

I twist my head to look at the woods and, in some faint part of my brain, consider making a run for it. The concept of running, no matter how remote, causes me to retch and I throw up a good portion of my drink.

I push myself up, wipe my mouth, and blow on my stinging hands. I'm partially aware of a wet sharp throb from my knees, but I don't need to ascertain the damage. I have an image of Le Loup sitting me down, cleaning my scrapes with peroxide and mercurochrome, and squatting down to put Band-Aids on my sore knees. The way a death-row inmate will be revived from a suicide attempt, even if he's to be put to death the next day.

The idea of Le Loup touching me, touching me in any way, propels me to the truck.

'Fist-kisses,' I say out loud, surprising myself. 'I want fist-kisses,' I say again, close my eyes, and knock the rhythmical knock on the truck door, as Pooh had done two years prior.

'Is that Sam?' calls a deep nondescript trucker voice. 'I only want Sam.'

'It's Sam.'

'C'mon in, then,' says the trucker.

I climb up and pull open the door. The driver's face is askew to me, buried in a map, just like last time. It's a different person, though, I'm fairly sure. This one also is wearing a vented nylon baseball cap, an expanded black flight jacket, and a nettlesome-looking patch of beard and mustache, but there's a decidedly delicate quality to him I can't quite put my finger on.

'Is Le Loup in there?' I point to the curtain hiding the private recesses of the cab.

The driver turns toward me, and a look of confusion crosses his face.

'You're Sam?'

I nod, staring at the curtain, ready for Le Loup to burst out like a stripper from a party cake.

'The one that was a saint?'

I nod again and begin to doubt whether Le Loup is back there. Maybe this guy is going to drive me to him, to another location, one where bodies are easier to dispose of.

'Shouldn't we get going? Get this thing over with?' I stare at the thick canvas hauler gloves on his hands.

'Well, yeah. We'll get going . . .' He shakes his head at me. 'You haven't had very good training. You can't be Sam.'

'What're you talking about? I've had training. I've had the best!'

'Well, the way you began your approach was not in the least stimulating. I mean, to paraphrase you, "Shouldn't we get going?" is not conducive foreplay.'

'Oh, so I have to fuck you first?'

'I really don't think you're Sam.' He shakes his head.

'I'm fucking Sam! Now, my high is wearin' out and I'd rather get this over with before that! So can we just move on to whatever?'

'Fine,' he says and crosses his legs in a very un-truck-driver manner, 'just as soon as I make sure I got the right one. Now you're the fourth boy they sent out to me, and I've asked for Sam every time. I'm not so sure I finally got Sam.' His head sways from side to side in an attempt to regard me from different angles. 'They told me Sam was indisposed.'

'I told you I'm Sam!' I shout and feel a distant urge to cry.

The driver nods his head, narrows his eyes into thinner slits, and rubs his briary chin. 'Okay . . .' he says, like someone staring at an abstract painting and finally starting to understand it. 'Tell me, has your hair changed in any way?'

'My hair?' I say and absently touch it, something I generally avoid doing, as I've never adjusted to the shock of feeling a rough bristly surface in the place of fluffy softness. I realize this must be a trucker that once came to be blessed by me. I've since tricked with a fair number of my former devotees, and none had ever recognized me. 'I used to have curls, long, golden.' I sigh. 'Yeah, that was me. Saint Sarah.'

'Saint Sarah?' He starts to laugh. 'Saint Sarah?!'

'Are you gonna take me to Le Loup now or what?'

'You want me to take you to Le Loup?'

'I don't care where you fucking take me,' I say and sit down on the metal cab floor, unable to stand any longer. I start to sob. 'I don't care.'

'How about home?' says another voice. I look up to see Pie, from The Doves, dressed in her full Japanese geisha regalia, holding the cab curtain open.

I shake my head, thinking, Damn, what did Stacey pour me!?

'I guess you're sure, Pie, huh?' says the trucker, whose voice, like a crazy bouncing ball, jumps from a guttural low to a lilting high in no time at all.

'I'm sure,' says the Pie apparition, 'though I see why you'd be confused.'

'All right then, I'm taking this mess off,' the trucker says with a feminine sway and begins to peel the fur off his face.

'I'm not feeling well,' I say and put my head between my legs.

I look up to see the trucker taking off his cap and letting down a tumble of luxurious honeyed hair.

'Oh, Christ,' I mumble, and dry heave as I watch the trucker transform into Sundae.

'I know I must look awful,' the Sundae mirage says. 'But not half as bad as you do. You look worse than a bear's bottom sewed up with barbed wire.'

'Honey, try not to vomit inside here.' The Pie ghost moves forward. 'This is a borrowed truck. And I know he'll forgive the lingering womanly scents, but not puke.' I hear the swishing noises of her gown as she comes closer. 'My-oh-my! I cannot believe it is you. Cherry?' She pats my shoulder. 'Cherry Vanilla?'

I raise my head slowly and look up at Pie. 'This is not . . . I'm not hallucinating?'

'Oh, baby!' Pie crouches down next to me. 'Oh, baby! What'd they do to you? What'd that Le Loup monster do?'

'What in the samhain did he do?!' Sundae echoes. I look over to see her stripping off the workmen gloves to reveal her dainty, perfectly manicured hands.

I grab hold of Pie like a baby monkey does its mama and bury my face inside the precious, tangerine-scented silk folds of her kimono.

'I know, I know,' she says and runs her hand through my hair.

Since Le Loup cut it off, I've not allowed anyone to touch my hair. I've suffered many beatings from tricks and Stacey for slapping hands off if a john attempted to touch my head to push it down.

'They can take hold of my ears like I'm a soup mug, but I won't let them touch my hair!' I had to explain to Stacey after every complaint. I eventually learned how to gracefully remove their hands and artfully guide them to my neck.

I let Pie stroke my hair, allowing her sensitive fingers to probe out and massage the keloid scars on my scalp from Le Loup's switchblade.

I must've cried for quite some time, because when I finally lift my face out of Pie's kimono, there's a long dark stain and it sloshes like a wet towel.

'Your poor hands,' Pie says, examining the ripped-up skin of my palms. 'We'll have to tend to those when we get well on the road.'

'Yeah, we better get out of here,' Sundae says. She has pulled off the heavy Ben Davis jeans, the flight jacket, and boots to reveal her usual cheerleader's outfit, though not a very showy one, a more functional uniform, one fitting for an escape.

'Yeah, we bought ninety minutes from that offensive little man.' Pie shakes her head in repugnance. 'And that time must be about up.'

'I told you we should've bought more time,' Sundae says, positioning herself back into the driver's seat. 'It ain't like he's expensive! No offense, Cherry, honey, but they are selling you way below market value.'

'How'd you find out I was here? Did Pooh call you?'

'I think that was the name Glad said called,' Sundae says, checking the map again, then folding it effortlessly into its original rectangular shape.

'What took y'all so long?' I say and blink successively to make sure they really are here.

'Glad wanted to wait until he found out when Le Loup would be away,' Pie says.

Sundae puts her cap back on, but with her hair fully flowing beneath it. 'Glad said we can easily handle a bunch of inbred mountain men. But he wouldn't send anyone to face down Le Loup.'

'Well, hopefully we won't have to face anyone down,' Pie says, and motions for me to lie on the truck floor between them. 'We're just going to creep out of here like a beetle on a tea leaf.'

'So, Le Loup is gone?'

'Yup!' they both say.

Sundae pulls out a pair of high heels tucked under her seat and slips them on. 'Proper driving shoes,' she says. 'Okay, here goes . . .' Sundae flicks a bunch of switches. 'Norm at the garage lent us and wired this baby so we can cruise out as quietly as' — she shoots a grin at Pie — 'a beetle on a tea leaf.'

Pie nods approvingly.

I wait for the truck's lights to flash on or for it to give that release of compressed air gasp, or the usual noisy tremble trucks make when started, like a giant waking from a fitful sleep, but as we begin to roll I am awed by the utter silence. 'Glad even paid for special shocks and mufflers,' Sundae whispers.

I look out the windshield and gasp as we head straight for a cluster of trees.

'Whoops.' Sundae giggles and gently stops the truck inches from impact. 'Glad had this place scouted. He knew we'd need these.' She takes out from the glove box a pair of goggles with brick thickness around the front. 'Glad borrowed these from one of our DEA clients.' She slips on the goggles. 'Night-seeing glasses . . .' She briefly fiddles with them. 'Oh, now I can see everything.' She restarts the truck.

I grip the seat as Sundae navigates past the trees and brambles. I hold my breath as we pull soundlessly onto the little broken road that leads to the highway. I turn to the side window and can see Stacey still sitting there, basking in the histrionics of his soaps.

'Oh, fuck! This is working!'

'Of course it is. Glad planned it. Would you like a drink?' Pie says.

'Fuck yeah!' I pat my pockets feeling for my flask and can't find it. I only find my raccoon penis bone stuck in my back pocket. I throw the bone down and search my pockets more. I realize in a moment of panic my flask must have dropped out of my pocket when I fell. For a split second I almost tell them to stop so I can retrieve it. 'Fuck!'

'Well, now you sure got yourself a pair of latrine lips!' Pie sighs and lifts a silver thermos.

Relief swells over me as she hands over a little silver lid cup. 'You've turned into such a . . .'

'Boy,' Sundae finishes for her. 'Oh! I'm sorry. I didn't mean to say that. I don't mean to insult you.'

Pie pours what looks like a nice warmed brown bourbon into the cup.

'I know,' I say. 'But I'm going home and things can go back to normal.'

'Sure they can,' Sundae says, overly cheery. 'Look, look out there . . .'

I look away from my drink and up to see the fluorescent lights of the Interstate glowing in the near distance.

'God, I wanna go home.' I take a sip of the drink and almost gag. 'What is that?' I say wiping my mouth.

'Plum tea. Homemade,' Pie says, looking puzzled, then hurt. 'I made it special for you. Plum is excellent for digestion and I figured you probably haven't been eating very well, this being the heart of ramps country, after all.'

'I have missed Bolly's cooking something fierce.'

'He was featured in *Gourmet* magazine not that long ago. Now they take reservations at The Doves. But of course all of Glad's are welcome any time and CB'd-in reservations get priority,' Pie explains.

'You don't have anything else to drink?'

'What, like whiskey? I knew I smelled that on you.'

'I could smell it before he even came in,' Sundae laughs. 'Naw, we don't have that. Just plum tea and biscuits!'

'Want a biscuit?' Pie reaches for a tin at her feet.

I shake my head no. I crave a drink. I need a drink to help me utter the words that have been on the edge of my tongue since I realized this was not all an illusion.

I clear my throat. 'So, how is Sarah? How is my mom?'

'Look, look!' Sundae jumps up in her seat. 'We made it!' The lights of the highway blaze and twinkle above us like a straightened halo. Sundae bounces again on her seat, and as she does so the five-inch heel of her sling-back, open-toed pump snaps off, causing her leg to skid out from under her, land on the gas, and lurch her forward to land forcefully on the truck's horn.

The bellow of the horn was the only item on that truck that had not been mechanically muted. It vibrated the truck with its endless bass trombone wail.

'I'm stuck!' Sundae screams over the horn's blare. 'I can't get my arm out!'

Pie leaps up and yanks at Sundae's arm that is somehow woven into the steering wheel as if it were a piece of macramé. They both stand and yank and yank till they tumble backward as Sundae's arm is released.

The silence as the horn blast stops is deafening.

'Let's get the fuck out of here,' Sundae says.

When I hear the distant air-raid siren, I am not surprised. I realize I'd been waiting for it the whole time. I just feel angry that I had actually let myself start to believe that I could go home.

I watch Pie's and Sundae's mouths yell in panic as the siren overcomes us like the scorch after a mine explosion. I watch them abandon their usual gently balanced lissome conduct and supplant it with precarious, rigidly hysterical movements.

'We have at least a good lead on them!' Sundae yells as if the horn were still bleating.

The truck roars around the mountainous curves, rocks flying like projectiles in its wake as the back wheels brush off the road.

'They're here!' Sundae says as if a home team had just scored a touchdown.

'I thought it would take longer for them to catch up to us,' Pie says, gathering her composure after gazing into the side mirror.

'Maybe you should just pull over and let me out,' I say, only able to imagine going back to find my flask, incapable of thinking beyond that.

'Fuck that!' Sundae says in a deeper, more masculine voice. 'I'm late for a date as it is!'

'Gimme that CB!' Pie says, also with a virile tonicity, and grabs the CB mike with a forceful poise I'd never imagined her capable of.

It dawns on me that their spastic, emotional display is like watching a metamorphic transformation in reverse. It's as if two butterflies were sucked backward into their cocoon to unravel into staid, solid caterpillars. I lean over to look in the rear mirror and can make out Stacey sitting shotgun in a red pickup truck behind us, his substantial head leaning out the window with his mouth stretched wide open like a dog howling at the wind.

'They're right on us,' I say, trying to keep a well of panic at bay.

I look again and notice another pickup right behind the first. I remember hearing Stacey caution us Le Loup paid a thousand dollars for the live recapture of any escaping lizards. And I also remember Stacey boasting how he had used a good portion of his various reward monies to tool up his truck so he could ensure more of those captures.

'There's no way we're gonna make it!' I say.

'Don't be such a boy,' Sundae admonishes me and swerves

the truck around a steep precipice as we make our way up Cheat Mountain.

Pie says into the CB handset, 'Break one-nine, break one-nine.'

'Go ahead, breaker,' comes the discarnate voice through the CB.

'This is Asia Cakes. Ninah Waya, you got your ears on?'

'That's big ten-four. What's your twenty?' broadcasts a different crackly male voice.

'I'm comin' up over the mountaintop, with a pick 'em-up convoy on our backdoor.'

'Yeah, roger.'

'Shit!' I shout as Stacey's truck pulls alongside us on the right.

'Our toenails are scratching and the four-wheeler just about blew my doors off,' Pie says into the mike.

'Roger,' says the disembodied voice again.

'He's got a rifle,' I cry out. Driving next to us, Stacey struggles to get his shotgun clear to aim at us.

'We got a pick 'em-up playin' duck season,' Pie says into the CB.

'Don't worry. He wouldn't dare to use a shotgun on the Interstate,' Sundae says, pulling the wheel tight around a curve, her petite muscles bulging.

'I lost my flask,' I say as calmly as I can manage. 'Maybe I can go back with them and get my flask and y'all can come get me later.'

The usually soft muscles of Pie's face pull into a clenched look of disbelief as her face turns toward me and then falls into a solid knot of sorrow, concern, and enough disappointment for me to feel so utterly lost and hopeless that all I can do is retch in response.

A loud blast, like an M-80, echoes around us.

'He's shooting out our wheels,' Sundae says matter-of-factly, 'which I find very rude, not to mention inappropriate, roadside behavior.'

She turns the wheel and slams our truck against Stacey's pickup.

'Uh, Ninah Waya, we got a situation here. Pick 'em-up is playing target practice on our skates, deeply offending Day of Rest's sensibilities, and now we're playing bumper cars, heading for a crack-'em-up.'

I watch Stacey's car swerve and the smell of burning rubber fills the air.

'Roger, Asia Cakes, you got a clean shot to yardstick forty-three to your drop stop and the chicken coop is all clean, copy.'

'Yeah, roger.'

A shotgun blast booms around us, followed by a loud poplike explosion. Our truck skids and brushes into the rocky pass on our side.

'We got a blowout from the ankle biter and we just dropped it off the shoulder,' Pie says into the microphone.

'Yeah, roger, what's your twenty?'

'Crossing the Pearly Gate soon. Gonna handle some business so goin' down and on the side.'

'Follow the stripes home with eighty-eights around the house.'

Pie hangs up the CB and stands up, impossibly balancing herself in the rocking cab. She gracefully raises her kimono to reveal a pair of black silk panties exquisitely embroidered with fire-shooting dragons.

Another shotgun blast sounds.

'That man is so ugly,' Sundae says, pointing out the window toward Stacey, 'he'd scare the shit off a pitchfork.' She rams his truck again. 'Pie, honey, I know a wild man gets the best of you, but this ain't the time,' Sundae laughs.

Pie smiles good-humoredly and proceeds to reach into her panties and dig between her legs. 'I'm very good at keeping my goods strapped down,' Pie says to me. 'And I know just when to whip them out too.' She pulls out a small, sleek gun, then digs into her kimono and produces a clip and snaps it into the gun.

Pie closes her kimono, leans out the window, and before I even realize it, she's fired off a whole round of shots. I hear wheels skidding and screeching.

Pie reaches into her underwear, produces another clip, and squeezes off another round.

'Both those trucks are now rolling on their hubcaps,' Pie declares and waves a graceful goodbye to them.

I pull myself up to see Stacey's driver trying to keep their truck under control with their front wheels blown out.

'I date a samurai that uses a Mini Glock forty-five. He says swords are outdated. He even fitted this one with night sight for me,' Pie says over her shoulder. 'Lord, I love to watch that man shoot,' she sighs and fires off a few more shots.

'Pie, it's coming up—the Pearly Gate. This is the do-or-die point,' Sundae says, her voice abnormally subdued.

Pie presses the gun to her side and for the first time looks concerned. I pull myself up and I see the Cheat Bridge looming ahead of us.

'Ready?' Sundae asks before the gray metal structure, slowing the truck like a bull pausing before an attack. Pie and I both nod, then we all take in as much air as we can, puffing out our cheeks like hoarding squirrels. We move cautiously onto the bridge.

We've all heard the tales of drivers never making it over the Cheat River.

Some say it's the spirit of all those pioneers who once crossed a calm and impassive Cheat River in wagons, only to have it jealously rise up and steal their futures under its choleric waves.

'Those drowned settlers ain't gonna lie there easy and let y'all just cross the leisurely way,' Glad would warn any of his lizards planning a trip over Cheat Bridge. 'Neither are all them In'ians that died putting that bridge up.'

We all heard the tales of the vehicles that, for no reason at all, just suddenly ran off the bridge and plunged down into the Cheat. No matter how high they raise the guardrails, no matter how much grip they spray on the traction bumps, and no matter how slow the speed limit, nothing could stop the dead of the Cheat bringing down more company.

All you could do was take ahold of your breath as you cross and hope the dead let you pass as one of their own. I heard it said those drivers that have to cross the Cheat Bridge as part of their regular run have developed extraordinary lung capacity to rival the great Houdini.

I look down and see the Cheat River below, tumbling over itself, sending bits of spray into the air like little jellyfish tentacles.

The truck vibrates along the metal traction nubs, making it harder to hold in my breath.

I look behind to see Stacey's truck pause at the start of the bridge. His whole face expands like a bagpipe as he also takes in a gasp of air.

I clutch hard onto the backs of the seats and give myself over to the bridge's vibrations, overwhelming all my body's natural sounds and senses.

Pie and Sundae are silent as well. Their red faces are set in grim determination to reach the other side without the aid of fresh oxygen.

I roll my eyes back up into my head and fight past the hum

of our wheels on the bridge, past the roar of the hungry currents below us, and past the moaning voices of all the dead calling out for their lost mamas and papas and babies with a wretchedness so devastating you're tricked into gasping for air in horror.

I see Sarah's face, as I cradled it once when she had stopped breathing, the needle still stuck in her arm, leaking like a red-ink pen. I held my breath as the paramedics worked on her until she rose with a sudden thrust like a seedling pushing its head up out of the dirt in a speeded-up nature film. She looked at me, her eyes wild with the secrets of death, and said, 'I came back for you.'

She never spoke those words again, even when she did always come back for me, claiming me nonchalantly like a forgotten scarf at a coat check from the various group homes or foster care in the various states I'd been relinquished to when a new marriage that had seemed promising turned as useless as the fruit of a poison sumac. In my head I assure the dead. My resolve to be with my mother is all the air my lungs require.

I open my eyes and see the ivory Turk's Cap lilies waving at the end of the bridge like a crowd of monks' white hoods bowing a somber surrender flag.

'Why do you always come back for me?' I had asked her once when she lay on the bed in the tenuous world of alcohol-induced consciousness.

She slowly rolled her head to me, flopped an arm over the back of my neck, and pulled me closer as if she were pulling in won poker chips. 'Everybody needs someone to know who they really are,' she laughed, and guided my head down to lie next to hers.

The white of the lilies grows as searing as the ache of the air pressing to escape my lungs.

'I know who you are,' I say, gasping, and let the lonely dead drag me down.

'We crossed the Cheat,' Pie says, holding my head in her lap.

I shake my head and realize we're still in the truck, still driving.

'You okay?' she asks and wipes her smooth fingertips across my forehead. 'You passed out. We shouldn't've let you hold your breath.'

'Did Stacey fall in the Cheat?' I ask.

'No such luck,' Sundae laughs. 'He's still driving somewhere behind us on his axles! But we're almost home, though. Look!' Sundae points.

Pie gives me a hand up, but instead of The Doves' pink neon sign I see yellow signs announcing a weigh station commanding all trucks to stop. As we drive on, flashing yellow lights inform us the station is closed.

'It's closed,' I tell Sundae, annoyed that she had promised me home.

Sundae slows and heads the truck into the station.

'They're gonna follow us in there,' I say, pointing to Stacey's trucks, small in the rearview mirror.

'I hope they do,' Sundae says with a grin.

We roll slowly through the empty lot.

I hear Stacey's shotgun flying off warning shots, which are too far back to hit us.

'Testy, testy, testy!' Sundae laughs and pulls the truck into a space under a dim fluorescent light and parks.

'That was more fun than a dog rolling on a dead frog,' Sundae says, and opens the cab door for Pie.

'Are you turning me back?' I say somewhat hopefully, unable to envision getting all the way back to The Doves on just plum tea.

'C'mon with me.' Pie motions for me to give her my hand. I lift it to her and am not surprised to see it has a slight tremor to it.

'I don't think that's from nerves,' says Sundae, seeing my hand.

I hear the scraping sound of what must be Stacey and his accompaniment driving on their flat wheels. I follow Pie out of the truck and into the gloomy darkness of the closed station. I don't see any other vehicles around, except for Stacey's pickups, which are heading right toward us. We walk fully exposed out into the desert openness of the lot. I'm holding Pie's hands and can feel the quivering spread throughout my body now.

'Stacey's gonna blow us out like melons on a fence,' I mumble to Pie.

'Sure he is, honey, sure he is.'

I hear Stacey's truck heading right toward us.

'Pardon me, ma'am?' Stacey shouts to us from his rolling truck.

'Yes?' Pie turns to face the oncoming truck. I step behind her in a rather weak attempt to hide. Stacey's braying laugh fills the lot. The trucks pull up next to us.

Stacey and his partner, a gas station worker from Three Crutches, get out of their truck.

'Hi.' I give Stacey a partial wave, which he ignores.

Like a dog hearing the clink of a can opener and licking its chops in wetted desire, just hearing the jingle of Stacey's big key ring hanging off his pants causes my throat to click in its dryness and sets my nose twitching in narcotic craving.

A look of incredulous incomprehension sits on Stacey's face. 'Ma'am. Sorry to disturb you,' he says with thinly veiled sarcasm, 'but I do believe you have something that belongs to me.' He motions his head toward me. His other truck comes to a screeching park next to his.

'What, this little trick babe?' Pie says, holding up my hand like a mother being informed her child had done some transgression.

The gas attendant is holding the rifle at his side and I notice his finger is firmly pressed on the trigger.

'Is the driver in the truck? I'd like a word with him,' Stacey says as if he were a school principal.

'Oh, I guess he's in the truck still,' Pie says and points to it.

Stacey looks at his partner in disbelief and lets out a cold hard laugh. Pie joins in, which stops Stacey cold.

'What's this about?' Stacey asks, his face gone icily stiff except for his jowls that still are recovering from the laugh. 'Maybe you can help me. You see, someone stole one of my boys, I get brung out in the middle of the night for a chase, my wheels got shot out, and now I'm standing here making small talk to some Oriental geisha like we're all heading to a picnic. *Voce e um maluco e tambem um sete um!*' Stacey says and sucks his teeth like the Portuguese soap villainess. I feel a weird twinge of pride that Stacey is able to get in a bit of sarcastic humor, not his usual strong point. His Portuguese language tapes are finally paying off.

'I'm so sorry about your wheels. But didn't you shoot first?' Pie asks, and I almost expect her to slap his wrist in admonishment.

'Honey, I don't know who you are, but you are now the property of Le Loup of Three Crutches. And *I* do not hit or shoot mares, but *Le Loup* has no such qualms, so you might want to practice your restraint now.'

Pie nods her head in a submissive geisha way.

'Now, let's go get that driver.' Stacey nods and the gas station man nudges us with the rifle in the direction of the truck Sundae is in.

We walk in silence. Just the clicking of the men's boots and the soft padding of Pie's geisha slippers, set against the soft breezes blowing refuse, and the assorted scamper of small mammals chasing after the garbage. It's too overcast to even discern any stars.

I want to make some gesture of apology to Pie but am numbed by an overwhelming feeling of responsibility for her now being captured too, and soon Sundae, and in most likelihood having to endure the same circuitous fate as me.

I determine myself to stoically brave my engulfing nausea and protect Pie and Sundae in any way I can. I squeeze Pie's hand in what I mean as a reassuring signal, but she thinks my hand is slipping out of her clutch, so she gives me a quick comforting squeeze.

We get to the truck door and Stacey steps beside us. The gas station man raises the rifle. 'Knock,' Stacey orders Pie.

Pie does her little bow and knocks.

There's no response. I wonder if Sundae escaped.

Stacey nods to Pie to knock again. She does and still there is no answer.

'Try the door,' Stacey orders Pie.

'Whatever you want, sir,' Pie says and pulls open the door.

There's a trucker sitting in the driver's seat, his face turned from us. At first I think it's Sundae, but the way the flight jacket strains at the shoulders makes me realize it's someone else.

'Put your hands up in the air and throw down your weapons,' Stacey repeats, just like he's heard said on all the cop shows.

'Now you know I couldn't do that,' says a familiar voice. My heart constricts, thinking it must be Le Loup playing a joke.

'I'm about to blow a new window in you, if you don't do as I say,' Stacey stomps.

'Do as you must,' says the voice.

'I'm not kidding! I'm gonna blow you out!' Stacey yells.

'Stacey, I'm gonna give you a clear shot. And after that it's my turn.' The driver turns and stands. It takes me a fuzzy bit to recognize Glad standing there, his huge raccoon penis bone proudly dangling around his neck between his two leather pouches.

'Glad?' Stacey says. 'Glad?' He pushes the gas attendant's gun down.

'This is my concern, Stacey. Now I wanted this to go peaceably, but you gave chase, so I had to step in. How you wanting to end this, Stacey?'

'Glad, I'm just, I'm just getting back one of Le Loup's.' Saying Le Loup's name visibly emboldens Stacey. 'I got to bring him back. What business is this of yours?'

'He's one of mine, Stacey. Now, you know a little of what I do to those that mess with one of mine . . .'

'He's yours? This is yours?' He points at me. 'You went to all this trouble to get this back?'

Glad nods solemnly without looking at me.

'He's yours. Le Loup might not be too happy 'bout it, but if you say he's yours then . . .'

'Good to see you again, Stacey.'

'You too, you too,' Stacey says dispassionately. 'Okay, well.' He waves at his men standing there looking bewildered. 'We gotta get back. Wouldn't think you would bother with that one.' He points to me again. 'He's as worthless as tits on a boar hog.' Stacey turns and starts to head off with his men.

Glad stands there watching their retreat and doesn't turn to look at me until Stacey's trucks disappear onto the Interstate. He looks me up and down, up and down, and finally shakes his head woefully.

'I wanted a bigger bone,' I say in an unsteady voice.

He nods.

'Looks like you got it,' he says.

I shake my head no.

'I need a drink bad,' I say weakly

He nods but says, 'You're gonna have to sick it out.'

I nod.

'I wanted to be a real lizard, like Sarah.'

'Looks like you got that,' he says, leaning down to lift me. He scoops me up and I let myself collapse into his arms.

I don't remember most of the ride back to The Doves. I just remember asking for drinks from Pie's thermos and spraying out a mouthful of plum tea every time.

I vividly remember the stories of Stacey. I saw them more than heard them. Glad's tale became graphic movies in my semi-hallucinating state.

Stacey had worked at the Doves. He was once one of Glad's star lizards. This was back seven years ago when Stacey was thin and lithe as a doe. I succeed in picturing Stacey with hair only to realize later I had actually visualized a hedgehog.

'Stacey won many a heart, was a sweet little girl,' Glad says. 'One day a young man had a date with Stacey and fell in love. He swept Stacey off with him to marry,' Glad sighs. 'Well, not a month later Stacey came back all bruised, crying, saying her husband had done sent her back. We welcomed her and all went back as it was.' Glad's voice gets restrained. 'Not too long after my girls started to get sick. Puke the color of pitch, eyes rolling back, barking like dogs, speaking in tongues. Folks started saying The Doves was cursed. That my magic was evil,' Glad grunts.

'Finally I sent for an old Choctaw medicine man. He looked at the girls, looked at their blue urine, and he knew. Somehow they were consuming poison. Someone was taking ground-up raccoon penis bone and giving it to my girls.' He shakes his head.

'Didn't take me but five minutes to spy on Stacey sitting there in her trailer, pouring out the powdered dick into the liquid lip gloss all the lizards bought from her for its luminous magical shine. Didn't take me but another fifteen minutes to find out her husband, who fancied himself a pimp, wanted to do in the competition.' Glad grinds his teeth as he talks. 'He was buying up every road kill, hunted, and pet store raccoon from here to Louisiana. I didn't let on I had found out. I just quietly got my girls to quit using Stacey's lip gloss. I gifted Stacey with a tin of the most irresistible fry breads, which she gobbled right up.' He claps his hands together. 'Well, the short of it is, I gave Stacey quite a dose there, mixed with a few other gifts from the medicine man. Blew up her balls as if she was a breeding bull.' Glad chuckles. 'I turned her back to her husband, knowing he couldn't just pretend his wife's genitalia weren't there any more, which is what I heard how he had handled it. That's how I know Stacey and that was my dealings with Le Loup, her husband.' Glad brushes his hands together as if smacking off dirt. 'That's why Le Loup makes a big production of proving his virility with all his female lizards. Makes it a goddamned holy celebration. I'm sorry you got to experience that,' Glad says to me.

I don't tell him I actually didn't. I don't say anything much at all, except to ask for a little can of shoe glue or maybe a little jug of some shine.

I lie in bed for a month recovering. I stay in Glad's trailer and eat Bolly's specially-made medicinal gourmet soups. My hair grows to graze my ears for the first time in almost two years.

Pie and Sundae visit to bring me books and entertain me with the humorous tales of their latest tricks.

Whenever I ask about Sarah, however, the subject is artfully changed.

Finally one night, when I feel strong enough, I slip out the window and run to the old Hurley motel. I stand outside our room door, examining the various kick marks, the old ones, some new ones. I listen at the door and strain to hear her sleeping breath. Every fiber in my body yearns for her, to tell her I am home. It feels like we are two magnets separated by a loose-leaf sheet. Finally I knock and, after no response, I ring.

I hear a man's voice, then a woman's, soft and muted. I ring again, harder, I kick at the door, bang it with my fists, till finally the door pulls open and I push past the man and run into the room. Our room. I dive onto the bed, where she lies under the covers.

I hear him roar in the background but ignore it and pull back the covers, climb in, and curl as tightly and as closely as I can to my naked mother.

I don't hear the shouts of the woman I lie against until the man rips me away and throws me against the wall. As his fists drive into me, I scream for her, on the bed, 'Momma, Momma, Momma!'

I wake up to find myself lying on a thin mattress in a jailhouse cell. My body feels like an amalgam of misplaced bones.

'So they've dropped the charges, Glad. He's yours to take.'

The cell door slides open and Glad stands there, looking at me with a sadness that burns through me like a fever.

'She's gone,' he says finally.

'I know.' I stare up at the cell's peeling-paint ceiling.

'She left with Mother Shapiro a good ten months ago. No one has heard from either one of them since.'

I nod.

'They went to California is all I know.'

'She always said she'd go there.' I move my head to look at the rectangular slit of a window in the middle of the cell wall, barred with broad old rusted iron slats and a thick pane of glass.

'It's not gonna work' — he looks at his shoes — 'you working for me, You're a different kind of lizard now.'

I nod. It amazes me that somehow those little light shafts still bother to squeeze through.

'You can stay with me for as long as you like, though.'

I nod. I raise my hands up toward the window.

'Here. Norm found this in his truck. It's your bone.' He leans over and places it in my raised hand.

I nod my thanks.

'It won't work.'

'I know,' I say and strain my arm up.

'You seem a lot like her, though,' he says with a smile, offering me a compliment that we both know is really not one.

'I feel a lot like her,' I say. 'I do.' I raise my hand higher, the bone wrapped in my palm, and watch the light dance over my fingertips.

Acknowledgments

My sincerest gratitude to all of the following:

My sisters of 465 Friendly Home for Girls, Akerman LLP, Irwin and Evelyn Albert and family, Jo-Jo Albert, Asia Argento, the Authors Guild and Jan Constantine, Amy Baker and Harper Perennial, Adrian Bartol, Julia Bernhardt, M.J. Bogatin, Will Brandt, Kurt Brungardt, Jose Luis Carreon-Macedo and Simple Cloud Works, Christelle de Castro, Lucas Celler, Godfrey Cheshire, Bill Clegg and the Clegg Agency, William Corgan, Deadwood Season 3, Justin Desmangles, Cheryl Edison, Judy Farkas, Grant Faulkner, Gina Forsythe, Leon Friedman, Uwe Gabel, Mary Gaitskill, Henny Garfunkel, Panagiotis Gianopoulos, Jane Gilday, Dr. Richard Glogau, Dr. Erica T. Goode, Carol Haas, Miranda Albert Haines, Chris Hanley and Muse Productions, Fayette Hauser, Laila Hayani, Sean Howell, Aïda Jones, Martha Keith, Todd Kessler, Noah Khoshbin, Julia Kim, Dr. Kevin Knopf, Dr. Josh Korman, Gretchen Koss, Katia Kulawick Assante, Kimberly Lau, Bruce LeRoy, Marie LeRoy (Vitalie), Jasmin Lim, Gary Lippman and Vera Szombathelyi, Paula Malcomson, Shirley Manson and Garbage, Maria Di Maruka, Tracy Marx, Beverly Mesch, David and Rita Milch and family, Andrew T. Miltenberg and Nesenoff Miltenberg

Goddard Laskowitz, LLP, Nancy Murdock, Dan F. Nicoletta, Lewis Nordan, Stella Okolue and the staff of 465 Friendly Home, Sharon Olds, Jess Owens and Jennifer Parkes and family, Dr. Terrence Owens, Levi Palmer, Diane Pernet and A Shaded View On Fashion, Barbara Petratos, Mike Potter, Carmelo Puglisi, Christine Rahimi, Nathaniel Rich, Karen Rinaldi, Noreen Ringlein, Lucinda Riva, Rudy Rivera, Roaring Mouse Cycles, Dr. Bruce Roberts and LightHearted Medicine, Mick Rock, Rock Point School, Joel Rose, Henry Rosenthal, Albert Sanchez, Karen Schulkin, Katrin Schumann, Johnny Silver, Smashing Pumpkins and Billy Corgan, Tom Spanbauer, Art Spiegelman, Michael Spring, Jerry Stahl, Jeff and Joan Stanford and family, The Stanford Inn Mendocino, Lauren Stauber, John Strausbaugh, Patti Sullivan and Jill Harris, Catherine Texier, Thomas Tillinghast and his vicious dogs, Joslin Van Arsdale, Gus Van Sant, Suzanne Vega, Eric S. Weinstein, Robert Wilson.

Special thanks to Nicole V. Gagné.

Love and gratitude to Donald David.

All my heart to Trevor Knoop.

AUTHOR: THE JT LEROY STORY is a documentary of the most explosive literary scandal of our time. It takes us down the infinitely fascinating rabbit hole of how Laura Albert—like a Cyrano de Bergerac on steroids—breathed not only words, but life, into her avatar for a decade.

Albert's epic and entertaining account plunges us into a glittery world of rock shows, fashion events, and the Cannes red carpet where LeRoy became a mysterious sensation. As she recounts this astonishing odyssey, Albert also reveals the intricate web spun by irrepressible creative forces within her. Her extended and layered JT LeRoy performance still infuriates many; but for Albert, channelling her brilliant fiction through another identity was the only possible path to self-expression.